D0881189

THE WORLD
IN
THE ATTIC

THE WORLD
IN
THE ATTIC

By

Wright Morris

A BISON BOOK

UNIVERSITY OF NEBRASKA PRESS · LINCOLN

9/1972
am lit

PS
3525
O 7475
W6
1971

FOR MY WIFE

Footfalls echo in the memory
Down the passage which we did not take
Towards the door we never opened
Into the rose-garden.

.   .   .

Other echoes
Inhabit the garden. Shall we follow?

T. S. ELIOT
"Burnt Norton"

BOOK ONE

THE WORLD

THE WORLD

"Where the smoke is———"

"What, Daddy?"

"Your father was born and raised," I said, and on what we call a rise of ground out here I stopped the car. That smoke was a train taking water in Junction, the smoke idle, like a dangling ribbon, but I seemed to hear the thunder the water made in the metal chute. When the train pulled out the water would drip on the dusty coal, making it shiny black, then on the tops of the cars, the cab of the caboose, and finally on the tracks. Thirty years ago it would also have dripped on me.

"For one thing—" my wife said, "there's too much sky."

Perhaps there was too much sky, in the winter like a rinse of bluing water, and in the summer like the faded bib of the old man's overalls. But if you want to get a rise out of me just tell me how you remember Nebraska as the place where you drove, all night, while the little woman slept in the seat.

"Three hundred years ago, son," I said, to make him acquainted with these matters, "a bunch of Spaniards on horseback came along here looking for gold. They had the notion there was a Golden City out here. I guess they passed within five or ten miles of where your Daddy was born." That made quite an impression, so I said, "At that time all of this country was a sea of grass."

"Isn't that grass out there now?"

"That's wheat," I said. "Can't you tell wheat from grass?" I turned my head and looked at the boy. Just thirty years ago, in another car, I had asked my father the same question, and he had answered it, word for word, the same way. It had been perfectly clear to me then—as it was to the boy in the seat behind me—that the man at the wheel didn't know what he was talking about.

"How can you tell?" the boy said.

"Don't put your Daddy over a barrel," said his mother.

"Anybody who was born and raised out here can tell you *that*," I said, and looked at the wheat, wondering what the difference was. That little question is quite a stickler, as you may know. As a small-town boy I couldn't really tell you the difference between spring wheat and grass, nor had I known, as a boy, what the country was really like. I lived right there in Junction, a flat island in the sea of corn. When I was eight years old my father drove me in a buggy to Grand Island, about twenty miles west, where he held my legs while I had my adenoids out. An hour or so later I was on my way home. I was put in the rear, where there was room to be sick and a large knothole in the floor of the buggy, where I could whoop-up, every half hour or so, all the grape juice I drank. I don't remember much about the country through which we passed. "That's all right, son," my father said, when he saw what I was up to, "if you're going to lose it you might as well taste it both ways."

Turning to his mother the boy said, "Is this God's country, Mummy, or is it still Daddy's?" In the rear-view mirror I could see his red face, the chapped lips, the peeling nose, and something like a button at the front of his open mouth. As he caught my eye he blew a blast on it.

"Where did he pick *that* up?" I said.

"Would it be from his father?" my wife said.

"I mean that whistle—where did he pick that up?"

"Ith not a withle—" the boy said, "ith a tain weel." As he talked it made its way to the back of his mouth.

"Are you going to let him swallow it?" she said.

"I'm here at the wheel," I said, and clutched it. My wife leaned over the seat and put her hand beneath the boy's chin.

"Now spit it out—" she said. The boy closed his eyes and washed it around, hungrily, in his mouth. He gave two long sucks, a whistle, then spit it out. As it dropped in my wife's hand I recognized it.

"Isn't that a button?" she said. I shook my head. "Then what in the world is it?"

"A train wheel," I said, as I could feel the boy's eyes on the back of my head. As I had often sucked on train wheels, my position was delicate.

"It's the wheel from a train," I said, "a toy train," and seemed to have the flavor right there in my mouth. But not as interesting as I remembered it.

"I suppose you know all about these things—" she said.

"Well, as a matter of fact," I said, then as I caught the boy's eye I thought better of it. "Stem-wind trains had loose wheels," I said, cryptically.

"Where did you get it, Honey?" she said.

"Cousin Ivy—" the girl said, "from his overalls pocket." A man of few words, like his father, the boy twisted his sister's arm and as she turned her back bit her, neatly,

[3]

between the shoulder blades. He favored the spot where the straps of her sunsuit crossed. Right at that moment a passing car threw gravel across the windshield, and we could see, through the dust, the crate of chickens riding on top. His sister stopped screaming, as she knows she can see more with her mouth closed. The white gravel dust hung over the road, sparking here and there like glints on a hitchbar, and when I closed my mouth I could taste it, like toothpowder, on my teeth. At the fork in the road there were sunflowers, a foot higher than my head, the broad leaves the color of the grass under the flour chute. The honey bee that crawled across the windshield was heavy with it. He dragged his stinger, like an anchor, till it caught on something. When I was a boy a kid named Bud Hibbard used to catch honey bees by swinging his cap, then pull the heads from the bodies, sip the jeweled drop of honey stored at the back. Then he would drop the heads to crawl about, aimlessly, in the grass.

"Well—" said my wife, "what are we waiting for?"

"I thought I'd let that dust settle," I said, "then I thought I'd show the boy what wheat is."

"He is not going to wade in that ditch, if that's what you're thinking," she said. "He can't sleep now from those awful jigger bites."

"His father is going to point out a few things for him," I said, and took the boy's hand, led him down the road. "Stand here," I said, "while your father picks you some wheat."

I could hear the metallic click of the big grasshoppers and see them glint in the air, going before me, then swaying the heads of the tall grass where they dropped. Sand burrs, still a little green and tough, stuck to my pants. At the bottom of the ditch I picked them off, rolling them softly between my fingers while I looked at the ditch, the earth cracked into a pattern like leaded glass. I think my father called this kind of soil Gumbo. A good word for it. When it was wet he drove the team—he couldn't keep the Overland on the road. Further down the ditch there was water, the color of lead poured out to cool, and where the dragon flies brushed it nothing happened, no circles formed. The sound I had been hearing was frogs—I turned to tell the boy. Thirty years ago my friend Bud Hibbard picked up a sand viper, swung him by the tail, and proved that snakes, after all, are quite a bit like the rest of us. That one threw up his lunch, which happened to be a frog. The frog looked very life-like, I thought, in better condition than the sand viper who remained at our feet, too sick to crawl away. We left them both there, I think, as we didn't feel any too good ourselves, and we stopped chewing the licorice cigarettes we had brought along.

"Oh, Son!" I called, as he wasn't standing where I had left him. When he didn't answer I climbed out of the ditch. He was down the road, twenty yards or so, but standing safely back from the edge of it to look at a boy on a black-and-white horse. When I was a boy we called them pintos, but I wouldn't go so far as to say that this was a pinto— or that pintos were a breed of horses.

"Your car stop?" this boy said, and for a moment my boy didn't answer. I think he was astonished to find that he understood.

"It didn't stop," he said, "my father made it stop." The boy on the horse smiled, gave his pony a pat on the rump.

[5]

He was a boy about twelve, I would say, with a round-moon face, well-spaced teeth, and as little neck as I used to have. He looked down the road at my car, then said—

"You know I don't know what I'd do without a black-and-white pony." Then he gave it a squeeze, with his legs, and they started off.

"Oh, Son!" I called, and he wheeled the horse around, looked at me. I suppose I called him just to keep him from going away. I didn't want to lose touch with a boy who could say something like that. "Could you tell me—" I said, "how far it is to the next town?"

"I suppose you'd like the biggest town?" he said.

"I think so," I said.

"The big one is Junction," he said, "that's about four miles." He looked at both of us, then he said, "Everybody ought to have a black-and-white pony." Then, "Well, I've got to go look after my cows." They were across the field, walking single-file around the grassed slope.

"The wheat surely looks fine, Son!" I said. God knows why, but I said it. He turned to see where I was looking.

"That's rye," he said, "wheat's over there." He pointed over our heads, and my son turned to look at it. Later he would remember what a fool his father was. I watched the boy ride away, a brown-and-white dog with a burr-heavy tail going before them, running ahead to check the cows at the open gate. As they came out on the road several of them turned to have a look at us. As if to see for themselves that fellow who didn't know wheat from rye.

"Is four miles out here far?" my boy said.

"You better ask your mother that," I said, and took his hand, led him back toward the car. I could see Peg leaning forward, the bobby pins in her mouth, to comb her hair in the rear-view mirror. There was some loose gravel in my shoes and I sat down on the bumper, loosened the laces, and tapped the gravel out in my hand. My father used to do that with the cinders he picked up along the tracks. He was an agent for the C. B. & Q., where he wore a green visor and black satin half-sleeves, and he walked along the tracks with a switch lantern every night. He would sit on the porch steps, out in back, with the lantern on the walk beside him, take off his shoes, and tap the loose cinders into his hand. Then he would carry his shoes, and the lantern, and walk around the house in his socks.

"How much do black-and-white horses run?" said the boy.

"If they run too much—" his sister said, leaning out of the car to speak to him, "they drink too fast and roll over dead."

"What have you been selling him now?" Peg said. "A black-and-white horse?"

"How are they on water?" said the boy, "do they run out?"

"You got to have water, Son," I said. "Everything out here depends on water. And when you want water you don't get it from a tap." I looked at the too-much sky and said, "Up there's where you have to look for water—that's why there's so much of it, and why it's so important out here." When I talk like that to the boy he listens to me.

"Does it rain when you pray or don't it?" the boy said.

"Or does-unt it!" said his sister.

"Sometimes it does, sometimes it does-unt," I said. I wiped the dirt off the windshield with a piece of Kleenex,

[7]

then walked around the car to see how the tires were standing up. I could remember when gravel was hell on tires. On a trip from Junction to Omaha my father and I once used eight tires. That was about nine miles per hour, and per tire, that is. I thought that the boy might like to hear about that but we were still four miles out of Junction, and I think his mother had heard it before, several times. I got in the car, released the brake, let her coast.

"If we're only four miles out," I said, "we can't be far from your Grandfather Osborn."

"Where's he?" said the girl.

"In the cemetery," I said. I meant that as a simple statement of fact, but I could see that my wife didn't.

"If that's your idea of humor," she said, "we can do without it until you feel better."

"She asked me a simple, direct question," I said, "and I gave her a simple, direct answer."

"Are you going to argue the point?" she said.

"Your Grandfather Osborn," I said, catching her eye in the rear-view mirror, "was quite a preacher, he used to sell Bibles from door to door. They say that when your Grandfather prayed for rain, it rained all night."

"Do you hear what you're saying?" Peg said.

"All I'm saying is—" I said, "what I was told. I was told that he prayed and it rained. What's wrong with that?"

"If it rains for forty days and forty nights I'd rather have a boat than a horse," said the boy. Nobody denied it. That settled that.

We crossed the Platte, where I described for the boy how most of the water flowed underground, which ex-

plained why such a wide river looked so dry. "Nebraska—"
I said, just in passing, "is an Indian word meaning shallow
river," a statement that once held a good deal of power
over me. It is linked in my mind with a Totem Pole, in
a park in Omaha, said to be carved by an Indian named
Cu-Yu, of a tribe now extinct. This fellow Cu-Yu, I'm
afraid, looms large in my private life.

"Is that it?" said my wife, and shaded her eyes from
the glare to look at the stones, of red and gray granite,
back from the road. A man with a horse-drawn mower was
cutting the grass. He wore a wide-brimmed straw, the
brim waving a blue shadow on his shoulders, and from the
spring seat of the mower a green bottle hung, sweeping the
grass. There was no breeze, but the whine of the mower
was a cool sound, like a barber's shears, and the smell of
the grass, heavy and sweet, hung in the air. Near the middle of the grounds was a pump, with an enameled pail
beneath the spout, and a man's denim jacket thrown over
the shaft, shading the pail.

"If you'd rather not stop," I said, "I'll pick up some
water, then we'll go on——"

"Since we're here," Peg said, "we might as well stop."

As I stopped the car the man on the mower raised his
hand, but without lifting his head, and I heard him call
out something to the horse.

"I don't suppose—" Peg said, "you remember where
he's at?"

"There's a plot," I said. "I think you'll find there's an
Osborn plot."

"Now remember—" Peg said, looking at the boy, "no
running up and down, no picking flowers, and if you have

to read, no reading out loud." Then she turned to me and said, "Clyde, where's that whistle?"

"It's a train wheel!" said the boy.

"Where is it?" his mother said. He looked at her, then at his father, then brought it up from the back of his mouth, blew on it, let it drop into his mother's hand.

"It tastes like face powder now, anyhow—" he said, and wiped his mouth.

Sometime before I was born out here my Grandfather Osborn had found it too crowded, hemmed in, as he said, by people on every side. Two or three in Junction, several more in Marquette just nine miles away. Neighborliness, in his mind, was a good day's drive. In the early seventies he built a house near the edge of the bluffs, overlooking the valley, with a tower on one corner and the hedges trained to grow to look like birds. People from Junction would drive out on Sunday for a look at it. He farmed week days, sold Bibles on Sunday, and sired eleven children, the seventh of them a little girl named Grace, my mother. But long before she had met my father, who was, as they said, a young man of caliber, the old man had decided that the state of Nebraska was too small for him. That the new frontier was too old for him. He went to Canada, northern Alberta, until he ran across some man up there, then his name appeared among those lost in the Galveston flood. Nobody who knew him took this report seriously. I didn't know him; I had given him up with a good deal of the past, and gone to Chicago, when I received a letter from Boise, Idaho. It was my grandfather's signature, but was written by my Aunt, one of his girls, and offered me the chance to go to college at his expense. The college he named was in California, and it didn't strike me as very important that it was run by people known as Seventh Day Adventists. That's another story, but on my way to this school I stopped off in Boise, Idaho, where I saw the old man for the first time. That winter he was eighty-six years old. He was a short, powerful man, wonderfully sound in body, but given to living too much alone. He lived by himself, farmed by himself, and the day that I was driven out to see him he had got up in the morning, at dawn, and hitched himself to the plow. He was there in the harness, the reins in his hands, when we came for him. The line between himself and the horse had disappeared. My Uncle Dwight was inclined to say that this line had never been very certain, and that the old fool—as he called him—had driven himself to death. Perhaps he had driven everything he could get his hands on. The woman he married, several he hadn't, his hired hands, his five sons and four daughters, and when they had left him he had driven himself. It could be said for him, anyhow, that he had not stopped there. When the time came, as he knew it would, he had put himself in the harness, hitched himself to the plow, and stood there with the reins in his hands. A madman, more than likely, mad all his life with the incurable vagueness, the receding promise, of the next frontier.

When I saw him his hands were still strong, clasping themselves for warmth when they were empty, and he sat by the fire with a blurred, foolish smile on his face.

Looking at me, wondering who in the world this stranger was. Was I his boy? They let it go that I was. There had been so many, how could an old man keep track of all of them? Across his brooding face, now and then, like fire-light, I thought I saw signs of recognition—not of me, but of himself, his new hopelessness. It was no easy thing to be the horse, and the rider, at the same time.

In his will, divided among his children, were the splintered fragments of three frontiers—Paradise won, Paradise lost, but never regained. Could you mark the spot of something like that with a stone?

"Here it is, Clyde—" my wife said, and stepped back from the stone to look at it. A large piece of gray granite, with a leaf-and-flower ornament. Between the flowers the fading inscription—

NEVERMORE TIRED

"Whoever thought of *that?*" my wife said.

"I suppose they all did—" I said, but I was thinking of my father, whose name was on the stone behind. In many ways I had not really seen my father until brought here, face to face with the stone, the dried flower wreath, and the fact that this huge piece of granite was tipped. That it stood before me like my father in his photographs. Erect, his heavy hands at his side, but somehow off the plumb line so that you tipped the photograph, or the album, to straighten him up. But an impression of him forever falling remained in my mind. With the album put away I saw him leaning, his arms flat at his sides, until he pitched forward, soundlessly, into the blurred fringe of grass in the yard. Now a long stem of grass waved a shadow over

[12]

his name, and the date, and I leaned over to pull it out as I walked by.

When I reached the gate the old man had unhitched the horse from the mower, and was backing her up, very slowly, between the shafts of a gig. A round honing stone, rough as a handshelled cob, stuck out through a hole in his rear pocket, and a grass-stained sickle was crooked in the belt at his waist.

"You an Osborn—?" he said, peering over the mare.

"Why—yes," I said. He waited and I said, "My name is Muncy, but my mother was an Osborn."

"If your mother was an Osborn, you're an Osborn," he said. He had raised his voice as if he was arguing with some one. He let it fall, spit, and looked me in the eye.

"I guess that makes me an Osborn, then—" I said. "You wouldn't happen to be from Junction?"

"What you mean—happen?"

"You're from Junction?" He signified that he was. "There used to be a Hibbard," I said, "a Bud Hibbard—" he waited for me to go on. "I just wondered if there were still any Hibbards around?"

"Any reason they shouldn't be?"

"You're a man who ought to know," I said, "—if you cut this grass very often. Don't the Hibbards die?"

"Some people doubt it," he said, and gave me a look which implied that I had touched on quite a subject. "Ayyee—yup," he said, and looked at Peg.

"Now what are you up to, Clyde?" she said.

"I was just asking this gentleman," I said, "how things were going with the Hibbards. Bud Hibbard was a friend of mine."

"If a Hibbard ever was, he still is," the old man said.

"We're just passing through," I said, "but if I thought Bud was still around——"

"Was this mornin'—" the old fool said, "likely still is." He tossed the reins over the splintered buckboard, climbed into the seat.

"Bud and I went to school together," I said, "you remember my tellin' you, Honey?"

"Is there any town in this state," she said, "you didn't go to school with somebody?" In the pause, I could hear the mare stomp in the dust. The old man slapped her with the reins, a dry sound on her hairless rump, where she was smooth as a boot and stained the color of tobacco juice. "Tch, tch—Dolly," he said, and she broke into an easy loaf.

As the boy followed me back to the pump I had another drink, although I wasn't thirsty, in order to show him how this was done when his father was a boy. Due to a certain miscalculation, and the improvement, I suppose, in pumps, I got us both pretty wet when the water shot out the top. But there was cold water at the spout, tasting of oil from the pump shaft, and I could see that the boy was favorably impressed.

My wife had dampened her handkerchief to wipe off the girl's face, and had run a comb through her short stubble hair. Back in Lone Tree my kids had got tangled up with flypaper, something new in their lives, and had to have every hair on their heads shaved off. Since that time they had got in the habit of wearing straw hats. They both looked fairly normal now, perhaps a little knobby from the rear, but nothing to frighten you if you stumbled on them in the dark.

[14]

"And who is this Bud Hibbard person?" my wife said.

"I told you," I said. "We were in the third and fourth grade together."

"Back in Ohio—" she said, "I was in school together with several hundred people. Did you consider stopping for one minute with any of them?"

"Bud Hibbard is an old friend of mine," I said. "We used to write quite a bit. I used to stop off and see him."

"When did you see him last?"

"In nineteen thirty-three," I said. That did it. That gave her something to think about. I drove out in the road, in the direction of Junction, and gave a toot on the horn when we passed the old man, his whip tassel up like flowering corn. A sign along the road said that Junction was not incorporated.

Nineteen thirty-three, you see, was the year I met my wife. We both stopped seeing quite a few people about that time. Bud Hibbard was one of them—I saw him the summer of that year, when I was on what we used to call a wanderjahr.

When I was a boy the Hibbards were what you might call a clan. They owned a good deal of property, gave a five-acre park to the city, and brought such things as UNCLE TOM'S CABIN to town. Through some Hibbard or other I was vaccinated, told to have my tonsils out. My father sometimes referred to it as Hibbardville, when we moved on to such places as Kearney, but all of that began to change, I guess, even before we moved. Like the Lone Tree Muncys, the Hibbards sired daughters—and nothing else. They were good-looking women, by and large, and either left town on their own, or on the arm of some Omaha boy with light-tan button shoes. Clinton Hibbard was the big man in my time, one of the big men west of the Missouri, and a man to father, as some people used to say, a county by himself. Perhaps he did, on the side, but the woman he married, a girl from southern Indiana, gave him nothing he could put the Hibbard label on. By nineteen thirty-three Clinton Hibbard was dead. My friend Bud Hibbard was the last man in the line. In some respects he was not much of a Hibbard, being a half foot short of six feet tall and not much to recommend, from a Hibbard point of view, what little there was. Somewhere I've got a snapshot of Bud showing him the day he graduated from High School, a little boy with horn-rimmed glasses, knee pants, and a pair of Ked basketball shoes. Two years later his father died and overnight he was a man, supporting his mother, wearing long pants now but with the blue serge coat in the photograph. I was not a man, that summer, but I was old enough, on my way to Europe, and according to the passport photograph what we call the clean-cut type. Not a man to go through Junction without looking up his old friends.

"We've got to eat somewhere, Peg—" I said, "why don't we have a bite to eat in Junction? While you and the kids are eating I'll peer around, have a look at Bud."

"That's fifteen years—" she said.

"What is?" I said.

"Since you've seen him," she said. "Fifteen years is quite a bit."

"I know what you're thinking," I said, "but I doubt if

Bud's changed. Fifteen years doesn't matter so much out here."

Was that true? What would Bud Hibbard say to that? If he lived in the same house I would say, turning from his face to look at the walls, "Well, Bud—it sure looks like old times." That would be true. I would be willing to bet on that. In the bedroom, where I would be standing, there would be the same dresser, the same drawers would stick, and the railroad poster of the Royal Gorge would be on the wall. The same people waving, perhaps their smiles a little faded, from the observation platform of the Overland Limited. Beneath the poster a length of twine—this might be gone now he was married—on which a curtain was suspended in front of clothes hung on the wall. Also behind the curtain a shelf of books, *The Pictorial History of the World,* and the book-like cases of select stereopticon cards. The instrument itself, with the velvet-lined hood, something like aviators' goggles, would be in the glass bookcase in the front room. In the parlor, as Mrs. Hibbard called it, under the glass-sealed case, would be a kind of diorama, showing the Lone Wolf under a starry winter sky. This was hand-painted, and the first work of art to enter my life. I think the deep case made the greatest impression, emphasizing, with two sheets of glass, the removal of art from the ordinary ways of life. Many years later, in college, I was amazed to find young men and women, merely human like myself, trying to do this sort of thing. People without this experience have missed an extraordinary handicap.

"I don't know what he's done," Peg said, "but I hope

[17]

you've changed a little bit." When I looked at her she said, "You've been married quite a while, you know."

"I know—" I said.

"Well, he's probably married too." She waited, then said, "Do I have to tell you what that can be like?"

I shook my head. I knew pretty well what that could be like. The last word I had from Bud Hibbard, some ten, twelve years ago, concerned itself with what he called the finest creature on God's earth. She had consented, it seemed, to marry him. I was not very broad-minded at that time, and I think I wrote him to the effect that that made it pretty tough on the rest of us. Sometime later, after a honeymoon in the Ozarks, he sent me a copy of *The Little Shepherd of Kingdom Come*. As I remember, our correspondence ended right there.

"We'll just idle by, Peg," I said. "I'm curious to see what the old town looks like."

"Is that a beer joint—" she said, "or a tourist camp?"

It was there on the highway, a block east of town. People from Lincoln, I suppose, were living in the cabins, as heavy lines of wash were strung up in the yard. The gasoline station, facing the road, had a nickel-plated Diner on one side, and a bar with a glass-brick window on the west. A Neon beer sign blinked on and off. Between the cabins and behind the bar were new post-war cars, some of them with trailers, but an old Buick touring was parked in front. A sack of laying mash was propped up in the front seat. As I made the turn at the tracks Peg said, "What's the connection between Junction—" she waved at it, "and a place like that?"

"Connection?" I said. "Does there have to be?"

I crossed the track and followed the creek at the edge of town. I didn't want to think about connections because right down the creek, where the bridge crossed, was the site of a very critical moment in my life. A girl named Evelyn had turned to me and said, "Kiss me." She was ten, I was going on nine years old at that time. "Kiss me," she said, and closed her eyes, pouted her lips—we had been eating blackberries—and after some time, it took me time to move, I had slapped her. Where I had slapped was like the skin of an apple, and when she opened her eyes I saw my own face, the mouth wide open, like a reflection at the bottom of a well. Then she turned and left me there, her panties showing as she ran off down the road.

"Maybe *you're* the connection," Peg said, but I wasn't listening, I was wondering if a man ever forgot the lover he failed to kiss.

"Your Daddy used to fish in this creek," I said. "What do you think of that?"

This road along the creek had more or less gone back to grass. There was grass down the middle and as we went along the big grasshoppers rose, with a chirping sound, then fell like a quick summer shower in the weeds. This sound went ahead of us like a brushfire, then closed in behind. But at the corner of the park the road had been graveled, the ditch grass mowed. In the brown house on the corner, in the dark front room, my father left his pants over the back of the chair and early Sunday mornings, quite early, I tiptoed into this room. The green blinds were drawn against the corner street light, and the morning sun. I would first have a look at the saucer on the dresser, among the collar studs and his ticking watch, then I would come back and slip my hand into his pants. The right leg pocket, where he kept his change. I would take a thin one and thick one, usually a dime and a nickel, though I sometimes slipped up on the thin one and turned up with six cents. Sunday afternoon, after church, I would blow it for Hershey bars. Under the front porch, behind the slat fence from where I could see out, but you couldn't see in, I would eat the chocolate and drink the red pop until I was sick. Then I would throw up and lie in the hammock till I felt all right.

"Is *that* the school?" my wife said, and I stopped when she pointed at it. It is quite possible that I have talked too much to my wife. That she has listened, all these years, a little too well. That worn building, of unfaced red brick, with the paper-flower cutouts in the tall, dark windows, was the wonderful place I seemed to have told her quite a bit about. My hand-scissored Easter rabbits were usually in the window on the right. At that time my father was going in for chickens, with several incubators going day and night, but some of these eggs, I'm afraid, never reached the chickie stage. Just before that happened I made rabbit eggs out of them. Sometimes very shortly before, with the result that Stella Conley, another girl I didn't kiss, found chickens in her basket instead of eggs. Her mother blamed this on my father, letting it be known that something like that might have made her pretty sick, but both my father and I saw her on the teeter-totter that same afternoon. She was there with Dean Cole, a boy who was known to have kissed them all.

"Is school still going on?" my wife said, and nodded at

the small dog asleep in the yard. One of these little terriers that my father always called a little fice.

"He probably thinks it is," I said, but I didn't go on to say why I thought so. Or why, perhaps, the dog always would. This same Dean Cole had such a dog, and when he went to Heaven, the year of the Flu, this little fice came to school every day looking for him. Then, thinking he had missed him, he went home again every night.

"How big were you, Daddy?" the boy said.

"Your Daddy was not very big," I said. "He had a seat near the map racks, down in front. But he was the one that told them about the Japanese Catastrophe."

"What do you mean?" Peg said, "*the* catastrophe?"

"I mean *the* catastrophe," I said, and seemed to see it before my eyes—the word CATASTROPHE, like a banner, across our Current Events. Facing the Fourth Grade class and Stella Conley, I said—"There has just been a great cat-ass-trophy—" at which point Mrs. Partridge came forward to lend me a hand. With her assistance I wrote it out on the board, parsed and accented, and along with the class, in what she called unison, we pronounced it half a dozen times. As I say, there has been just one Japanese catastrophe. The last one, God knows, calls for a better word than the one I chalked up on the blackboard thirty years ago.

"This is Hibbard Park, Honey—" I said, and looked through the trees, the idle chains on the swings, to where a Civil War cannon, with a seat-polished breech, sparked in the sun. The carriage wheels were still faintly red, and on each side, in a pyramid, were the cannon balls. On the top ball, under the stove-black, was the inscription—

C. MUNCY
IS A
LITTEL FART

On the lower balls, and on the door of Mr. Clinton Hibbard's new privy, was the name of B. Hibbard, compliments of C. Muncy. On this same door, inside, where time could be found for meditation, B. Hibbard had carved the following—

OMAHA SPAGETTI IS SOLD IN ITALY

C. Muncy spent one summer pondering that. Like Cu-Yu, the extinct Indian, B. Hibbard once spoke a cryptic lanuage, the key to which, once lost, was never regained. What horizons once loomed in Italy? It was twenty years before C. Muncy saw as far, if not so clearly, but by that time B. Hibbard had given it up. Whatever it was he had, or had seen, he had given it up.

"If you want to moon around," Peg said, "you might let us out where we can eat." She looked at me and said, "I suppose there is a place to eat?"

"Used to be a very nice place," I said, "called The Red Mill." I made the turn around the park, started back. Thirty years ago, I seemed to remember, Junction was an up-and-coming town with a new Depot, a water tower, and a Hotel on the American plan. A new National Bank, a new City Hall said to be as fine as anything they imported, with an office for the Sheriff and room for the Fire Wagon on the first floor. There were two or three restaurants, and one of them was Japanese. The Red Mill came along with the war, when things were looking up, pretty generally, like the Dutch boys and girls skating on the walls of the Red Mill. There were booths inside, where a man could sit with his wife and kids, and go about eating, without sitting in the open, at a table, with the yokels staring at you. My father considered himself a city man. When he wanted a wife, it was to Omaha he went for her. When he built her a home, it was a big, Omaha house. A mile out in the country, without a tree, or a neighboring house to protect it, but for all that an Omaha house, with twelve rooms, and one of the best. A city-bred man, one accustomed to city refinements, meals without bread, and never at a loss as to when to Table-dote, when to ala Carte. At ease with knife and fork alike. A man who could work, when he wanted, the candy machines on the back of the seats, or the magic violin, with the pink wax hand, in the glass case. This was ten cents, and I was given the coin to drop in the slot. My father was courting at that time, and the only thing to offer a fine city woman, an Omaha-bred girl, was Japanese food and the magic violin. In the summer when the door stood open, the violin could be seen from the street, or from the seat of buggies drawn up to the curb. With the coin in my hand I would look through the screen at the country boys, with their feet on the buckboard, and the light from the popcorn burner sparking their eyes. The violin would play, and my new mother, who had a nice voice, would sing—

> When you wore a tulip, a sweet yellow tulip, and I wore a big red rose———

She was very young, and my father was said to be very old.

"Is this the place?" my wife said. It was not the Red

Mill. On one side of the window was the word POOL, and though the glued-on letters were gone the shadows were faintly outlined with light. On the other side of the door was MABEL'S LUNCH. I looked down the street for THE RED MILL, through the high-noon glare on the vacant corner, the weeds gone, but still vacant, and the gasoline shack at the back of the lot. Beyond the corner, turned away from the gas pumps, the new development and Mabel's Lunch, was a row of stores facing the burned ditch grass—and nothing else. Like a row of old men with blinded eyes lined up to be shot. Down the spur of tracks was the cattle loader, the abandoned sorghum mill, and the coach house with the flight of stairs on the side. The stairs were gone, but the door on the landing stood half open, facing the town. I had seen women with large feathered hats and plush velvet gowns step from that door and lift their skirts as they came out on the landing and walked down the stairs. Showing more, as I remember, than the tops of their high button shoes. Sometimes they would pass right through the town, like a maverick circus wagon, on their way to the west-bound caboose, a half mile east. The east-bound caboose stopped right at the door. Sometimes the ladies out on the roof with towels around their shoulders, drying their hair, would yawp at the lady on the platform of the caboose. Sometimes the lady would yawp at them. With my own eyes I had seen such a beauty turn her backside to the coach house, and flip her skirts till the calves of her legs showed. Or with her long black-gloved hands, double-thumb her nose.

"You see it down there?" Peg said, and leaned out of the car to see for herself. Where the Red Mill had been the windows were green with blinds. The letter P, of an A & P, was still on the glass of the store near the corner, but the words ARMY SURPLUS were painted over the door. A black cat lay asleep in a box of boot socks.

"I guess the Red Mill folded—" I said, and parked the car facing Mabel's Lunch, and a woman with folded arms who stood at the screen. It was pretty hot, but she seemed to be hugging herself. Her shoes were unlaced, and the ball of each foot, like a white glass egg, plugged an egg-shaped hole cut in the side. As I backed from the car she pushed on the screen, fanned out a fly with her soiled apron, then turned and called,

"Ohhh Mabell—here's New York!" As my wife looked up the screen slammed, and the woman was gone.

Mabel's Lunch stood along one wall of a wide room, once a Pool Hall, with the empty cue racks along the back side. Beneath the racks were wire-back chairs, one of them piled with magazines, and between every third or fourth chair a brass spittoon. Near the center of the room, revolving slowly as if the idle air was water, a large propeller fan suspended from the pressed tin ceiling. It made a humming sound, like a telephone pole, or an idle, throbbing locomotive, and although the switch cord vibrated it was cluttered with flies. At the back of the room, on the Lunch side, an oblong square was cut in the wall and a large woman with a soft, round face peered through at us. After wiping her hands she placed her heavy arms, as if they tired her, on the shelf.

"I got a table," she said, "if you'd like me to put it up."

"Oh, no, the counter's fine," I said, and sat myself on

a stool, my arms on the counter, as I suddenly felt a little weak. In the past two hours I had felt it quite a bit. Something I might call home-town nausea. I can get it in a lunch room like this, or at the bend of a road, any country road, where a telephone pole tips out of a clutter of dust-heavy weeds. Or a track crossing, where you lean out to peer into nowhere, in both directions, the rails a long blur with the hot air, like smoke, flowing up. At such times it's hard to tell where the nostalgia stops, the nausea begins. While you're in the grip of one, the other one sets in. Before you know it you're whipped, you're down and out, you're sick with small-town-Sunday-afternoon. This sickness is in your blood, like a latent fever, a compound of all those summer afternoons, all those fly-cluttered screens, and all those Sunday papers scattered on the floor. The idle curtains at the open windows, the heat over the road like a band of light, and the man on the davenport, with his pants unbuttoned, the comics over his face. The dog who wants in, the cat who wants out, the smothered sound of dishes under soapy water, and the smell of chicken gravy when you lift your fingers to your nose. Everything is there in the hot afternoon, there in the room and at the open window, everything is there, in abundance, to make life possible. But very little is there to make it tolerable. Any one of these things, at a time, is nostalgia —but taken together, in a single lump, it is home-town nausea—you are sicker than you think. You had better sit down.

"I think I'd like some ice coffee—" I said. "I don't think I'll eat."

The woman who stood before me said to my wife, "I

can give you roast beef, roast pork, or meat loaf." She unfolded her arms, then folded them again, comforting herself.

"I think a sandwich is enough," my wife said. "Say you make it three roast beef sandwiches."

"There's four of you," said the woman. "Don't one of you eat?"

"My husband said he didn't think he would eat," she said.

When the woman looked at me I smiled and said, "I think I'll have just a glass of ice coffee."

"You wanta Seltzer, Mister?"

"No—no, thanks," I said. "Just some ice coffee."

She had started away. She turned back and said, "What was that?"

"Ice coffee—" I said, and wiped my forehead with the sleeve of my shirt. "I guess I'm a little hot."

The woman looked at me, then she looked down the counter at the face framed in the opening. After a moment, she looked back at my wife.

"Missus—" she said, "your husband pullin' my leg?"

My wife looked at me. "What are you up to?" she said.

"I asked for a glass of ice coffee," I said. I looked at the woman.

"What you mean by that?"

"Maybe I mean coffee with ice in it," I said.

"Now, now—" said my wife; then she said, "All he wants is some coffee with a piece of ice in it." She smiled at the woman. "You know, just a plain piece of ice."

"He wants it like that?"

"That's the way he likes it," my wife said.

[27]

The woman shifted her arms, looked at me for some time.

"Can we eat while you think this over?" I said.

"You said you didn't want to eat," she said. She looked at my wife. "You mind my askin' where you people from?"

"My husband is from *here*—" my wife said, and smiled sweetly. "I thought that explained everything."

"This man is from here?" I saw my wife's head nodding.

"Just bring him that ice and coffee," she said. "He'll be all right."

The woman turned and started toward the back. It was quite a little walk, twenty yards or so, and near the end she was hustling. "Oh, Mabel—" she said, and pushed through the swinging door.

I sat there without saying anything. Because of the length of the counter the stools were four or five feet apart, so we sat alone, in our own fashion, brooding over events. I had the feeling that the room seemed to magnify everything I said. Like voices in an indoor swimming pool. There were no curtains at the front windows but I was unable to see the street—the light stood there like a wall, a sheet of frosted glass. Behind the counter, in a pyramid, were several kinds of breakfast food, all of them bran, all of them guaranteed to keep you regular. The door at the rear opened again, and the woman came in, with a large tray, stopping in front of my wife to distribute the sandwiches. Then, at arm's length, she placed a cup of hot coffee in front of me.

"I understand you want ice in that?" she said.

"If you please," I said.

From a cereal bowl on the tray she scooped a small piece

of ice. It dripped on the counter as she leaned forward, dropped it in the cup. There were a few bubbles, then nothing—like a drowning man.

"Hmmmpphh—" she said, and leaned back, the better to size me up once more, then slowly, the tray dangling, started away.

"Could I trouble you for a glass?" I said.

She wheeled around. "A glass—my heavens what'll you think of next?" She threw up her hands, the tray slapping on her sides. The whole thing got the better of her and she leaned on the counter, propped on her arms, her head turned away to giggle into her sleeve. I kept my eyes straight ahead, on the breakfast food. When the woman was able to walk she made her way down the counter, rocking, and I found myself reading the small sign on the wall.

DON'T GO AWAY MAD—

JUST GO AWAY

it read. I raised my eyes, I went up the wall like a fly, to the pressed tin ceiling, then I went along the ceiling to a spot right over my head. There was a very small card—I strained to make it out.

WHAT THE HELL YOU LOOKIN' UP HERE FOR?

it said. I lowered my eyes, and took a swallow of the stuff in the cup.

"Honey—" I said, "I'm going to take a little look around."

"Now Clyde—" she said, a word she only uses at a critical time, but this time I felt a little critical myself. I stopped at the door and took a soiled toothpick from a whiskey glass. There was a box of King Edward cigars on the counter and I took one, bit off the tip, and slipped a dollar bill under the rubber coin mat.

"Can Daddy smoke cigars?" my boy said.

"No," his mother said.

With the cigar in my hand I walked out to the curb, looked up and down the street.

I stopped to scratch a match on the peeling barber-pole. The last time I had smoked a cigar was on 45th and Madison Avenue, where I had decided to have a good smoke, instead of my lunch. I very nearly died before I got home. Home was just across the river in Brooklyn, in Columbia Heights, but I sat in the basement of the St. George Hotel, on an elevator stool, for a little better than an hour and a half. When the elevator stopped I could see my face, apple-green with a fine Neon pallor, in the glass doors when they opened and closed. "Now you jes set there—" the operator said, a man who admitted, several days later, that he recognized the symptoms as he had once lunched on a fine cigar himself.

"Oh, well—" I said to myself, and lit the cigar.

Through the smoke I read the words A. BEGGS—BARBER, painted on the barber pole. Through the screen, puffed at the bottom where small boys leaned on it, I could see Mr. Beggs asleep in his barber chair. He faced the street—he had cranked himself around and pumped the chair up, as high as it would go, so that he looked like a man pumped up for a grease job. From that elevation he could see over the potted plants, at the front of the shop, and the soiled half-curtain that kept certain people from peering in. Without lifting his head, Mr. Beggs had a fine view of the street. If there was nothing in the street he could look at the tracks, the iron-wheeled baggage trucks, and the sign reading JUNCTION, EL 1,785. Beyond the tracks, and the trough of burned grass known as the railroad's right of way, was Route 17, the main highway east and west. One block down the highway, the WEE BLUE INN, the post-war white man's gypsy encampment, open all night, twinkling with car lights and Neon signs. Neither out of the town, nor in it, like those freight cars of circus people, parked along the siding, when Hagenbeck and Wallace come to town. Something of a menace, some people would say, and something of a distraction at the same time.

Mr. Beggs could see it all, and report on it. The cars that parked in front, using the bar, and the cars that parked behind, using the cabins. A sentinel, with an eye on the enemy's camp. The men who sat on the benches along the wall, one leg crossed over the other, their straws on the hat-tree, deserved an accounting of just what it was that was going on. They relied on Mr. Beggs, a man who had seen with his own two eyes William Jennings Bryan, and could tell you that men of that caliber were not turning up anymore. That is to say that Mr. Beggs—a man who could give you a word like *sugan*, which was Spanish for quilt, a man who came up from Texas in '96 with two thousand head of cattle for Wyoming—that is to say that Mr. Beggs, and men of that ilk, were not turning up. Mr. A. Beggs and the man, or men, seated along the wall, on the hardwood benches, beneath the calendars from Shenandoah, Coon Rapids, and South Omaha. Men who faced the gum machine, with the pink-and-white balls, Mr. Beggs, tapping his comb on his sleeve, and the extra barber chair with the towels in the seat and the crank wired down. Measures taken to keep the younger generation from killing themselves. Men like that, so to speak, were getting harder to find. Times changed—a Cold Wave fan stirred the tufts of unswept hair on the floor, and two of the calendars advertised something called hybrid corn. But the men—was it going to be necessary to change that? It was enough to make you wonder. Mr. Beggs did. He had time for that.

Times changed all right. In the weeds between the barber shop and the gas pumps, on the corner, were the carriage wheels of the old fire hose. Behind the wheels, facing away, a rear view of the water sprinkler, the buckboard seat riding high and wide at the front. On the rear of the tank, in faded yellow and green, a spirited example of the sign painter's art—

Visit The
L Y R I C
To Nite

In the window I could see that the man walking up behind me was not Beggs. But he had a barber's eye for the stranger, the new detail.

"Your name's Muncy?"

When I turned to look at him his hands were up, cupped before his face, lighting a stub of cigar. He wore black linen cuffs to protect his sleeves, and in his linen vest were several indelible pencils. As he blew out the match I saw the purple stain on his fingers.

"Yes, my name's Muncy," I said, and he stepped back a pace, his arms crossed, to look at me through a cloud of smoke. He was a wiry, bandy-legged little man.

"Mabel called me to ask what it was I wanted, told her—then she said, Leo, you remember anybody Muncy around here? Muncy, I said, well now, Chicken Muncy? I said. I don't know, she said, but there's a Muncy here now who says he's from here. Then I come out—" he nodded toward the bank, in the shadow across the street, "then I stepped out for my lunch, saw you here."

"Well, I guess that's me," I said.

"Knew your daddy well, loaned him money when he and Grace—that was your mother, we all knew her—went out to Frisco on their honeymoon. Took a boat ride somewhere. Guess they was pretty sick."

"That was before my time," I said.

"Indeed it was—yes," he said. "I guess it was." He examined the stub of his cigar, then said, "Tryin' to figure why I don't remember his family——"

"You mean me?" I said.

"That's right."

"Well, I wasn't born here," I said. "By the time I came along we were down at Lone Tree." I looked down the tracks.

"By George," he said, "that's right. Will was down at Lone Tree. Don't remember what he did down there—besides you—but that's where he was."

"Yes—" I said, "I guess I'm first of all a Lone Tree boy."

"Oh, well," he said, "there's not a whole lot of dif-ference—you think there is?" He looked down the tracks toward it, then said, "Might be a little now, don't think there was then."

"You think there is now?"

"Well, we've both slowed down some," he said. He looked across at the bank, the front said to have been of imported Italian marble, but the sides, one side, of unfaced red brick. Another building was supposed to have gone up there. Now there were two cars, one of them with a FOR SALE sign.

"Who's at the station now?" I said, as a man stepped out of it and crossed the tracks. He walked along the tracks toward the two freight cars parked near the tank.

"Potter—" he said, "think your daddy knew him." He stopped, then said, "But he wouldn't like it now."

"No—?" I said.

"Your daddy was a go-getter. It's pretty quiet now." A big double-header trailer passed on the highway, the tires whining on the concrete, but it was quiet along the tracks, up and down Main street, and on the road into town. Very quiet. I could hear pigeons crossing the tin roof of the barber shop.

"What's looking up—particularly?" I said, and he turned from the highway to look at the town. He took a step to the right to see beyond the water sprinkler.

"Mrs. Hall's doin' all right—" he said, and waved his cigar toward the head of the alley. I could see a large house behind the elms shading the street. At the front of the house, strung on a wire between the two hitching posts, was a sign reading TOURISTS, and below it—NO VACANCY.

"Are there people passing through—here?" I said.

"Well, she's always full up," he said. "She's got a sign down the road. See somebody pull into the yard every night. Camp across the tracks full of people workin' in Grand Island." He paused, then said, "City people, I guess—most of them."

At the door to Mabel's Lunch room an apron waved, dropped again.

"That's Mabel," he said, "guess she's ready for me."

"You mind telling my wife," I said, "I'll be gone for another ten minutes."

"Glad to. Mabel says she's a mighty purty girl——"

"Well, thanks—" I said. "You might tell her that, too, while you're at it."

"By George—" he said, sparking, "don't think for a moment I'm not liable to." While he grinned at me I could hear his fingers snapping. He turned away—then he swung back and said, "Young man, your mother was a mighty purty woman, an' if I'd had my way—" he paused, "your Daddy wouldn't be dead!" He did a tit-tat-toe, heel and toe, snapped his fingers, then pushed through the screen.

As I crossed the street, A. Beggs, barber, had his eye on me. His face was lathered, and in his right hand, like a mechanical bird, he held his winged razor—in the palm of his left hand, like a votive offering, the peppered lather from the blade. As I peered in he honed the blade on the heel of his hand. His lips were puckered, his eyes wide, as if the man who faced him in the mirror had kissed him, slapped him, or whispered something unprintable. I raised my hand, and as he waved his razor—a semaphore flick of the wrist—I remembered why I had been shaving myself, since an early age.

I cut across the empty lot where a cow was tethered, a small black Swiss, buzzing with flies, her dung-heavy tail thumping her sides like a bell-clapper. Gnats squirmed like maggots at the rims of her eyes. Just thirty years ago, on the Fourth of July, the citizens of Junction had burned the Kaiser Devil, the Beast of Berlin, on the spot where the Swiss now cropped the weeds. That afternoon we had marched the length of the town in step with a bohemian band from Schuyler, right behind Uncle Billie, who had the Beast of Berlin on a long clothes pole. This Beast was Mrs. Riddlemosher's scarecrow, with a kerosene funnel for a helmet, and he was burned on old egg crates, compliments of Will Muncy & Son. While the Kaiser burned the band played—with the exception of what was known as the wind section, as these men blew a little, but spent most of their time wetting their lips. They wet their lips, they fingered their keys, and now and then they blew out a great deal of saliva while they watched Bud Hibbard, who was very fond of lemons, sucking on one. I was not so fond of lemons but I was there, with a raw one in my hand, when a gentleman with white flannel pants led us away. That was Mr. Clinton Hibbard—Miss Caddy's man —and he gave us ten cents apiece to stop sucking lemons and eat popcorn instead.

In the door of the creamery a big fellow in tight overalls, and red rubber boots, slipped his hand into the slit at the side of his pants, bent slightly at the knees. His hand went far down, his eyes closed, and while he slowly scratched himself his knees flexed, up and down, like a man about to spring.

I heard the whistle, blowing thin and wild, before I noticed the man in the tower, his head bobbing like a toy, cranking down the gates. They bobbed for a moment, like corks, the red lanterns at the tips swinging, then they came down as the bell began to ring. Beyond the gates, on the far side of the tracks, an old man in a red-wheeled buggy braced his feet on the buckboard, drew up his mare. She stomped the road, the dust rising in a soft, sparking cloud, through which I could see the old man's shellacked straw, the reins taut in his hands. As the dust cleared he braced himself, ready for anything. She whistled again, then she went by with the white plume flat, the full length of the boiler, and I remembered how the whistle followed number 9 down the tracks. I saw the jacket of a porter, like a quick smile, flashing between the coaches, then she was gone leaving a vacuum between the gates. There seemed to be an open pit, the dust rising from far below, where there had been an explosion—later we would hear the roar of it, but it was quiet now. As the gates went up the buggy looked like the entrance to a mine.

"Was that number Nine?" I said. The man in the tower, a nail in his mouth, leaned in the window and peered down the tracks. The visor he wore cast a green shadow on his yellow face. He took the nail out, spit, and said—

"Nope, that was number Seven." He examined the head of the nail, put it back in his mouth.

"Didn't that used to stop?" I said.

"It don't anymore," he said. Then he seemed to hear, for the first time, what I had said. "You down here from the city?" he said.

"No—I'm from *here*," I said, and cut to the left, walking on the ties. I went along ten, fifteen steps, then I tried the rails.

"Nope, you're not from here," the fellow called. When I looked back he was picking at a front tooth with the nail. He found something, spit it out, then said, "If you was from here you'd never walk on the ties. You'd never do that—" he said, his head wagging, "not if you was from here."

I walked in the cinders, trying to think what it was that walking in cinders made me think of—something connected with walking the rails, or walking the ties. The weedy spur curved in behind the station, the semaphore shadow lying on the tracks, and I stopped in the shadow to look through the door into the Waiting Room. The great pot-bellied stove, the VOLCANO, was still there. Above the stove was the arrangement for trapping the heat—as my father said—generally used for drying wet shoes, coats and gloves. Underneath, on the stove board, the long poker and the crank for shaking down the ashes. The drafts were open, the damper in the elbow-joint half closed. On the wall behind the stove, thumb-tacked above the bench, was a facsimile War Bond made out to John Doe, the word "boy" carefully added to the Doe. On the side wall the wooden slat grill was still the cage around the ticket office, but the ticket window, where my father stood, was closed. I walked from the back of the station to the front.

In the old stations the agent's desk sat at the front, in a bay of windows, so that he could sit there and look in either direction, up and down the tracks. The big window at the front would usually be closed, against the noise and blast of the Mail train, but my father liked to keep the small windows at the side halfway up. That was for him to see out, and for me to see in. From a block down the tracks I could see his face, light green from the visor shadow, and hear the click as he worked the telegraph key. There would be a lamp over his desk, with a glass shade the color of his visor, and the metal freight tags on a wire near the wall. I could see them, glinting in the light, and the rack that held the dozen rubber stamps, some of them with labels, some of them that had to be stamped to be read. I could see through one window and out the other, far down the tracks to the cattle loader, where at 9:17 the semaphore would switch from red to green. And my father would rise from his desk and with the length of bamboo, with the loop in the end, stand out in front for the pick-up from the Fast Mail.

That window was down, but when I shaded my face, pressed my nose to the glass, I could see my father, the dark ridge along his forehead, sitting there. His right hand, with the "indelible" fingers, relaxed beside the small black key, and a purple stain, like a birthmark, where he moistened the pencils with his lips.

My father was not a man who could turn boys into lads by putting his hand on their heads, but he had known such men, and he had passed the faith on to me. Men like that, he gave me to understand, were a passing thing. They are tied up in my mind with the old Harvey Houses, where my father liked to eat, and where men of that stamp would sit at the counter, smoking their cigars. Their heavy cowhide luggage on the floor beside them, with the colored labels of faraway Hotels, and a way of saying— "Will, is that your boy?" that made a man of me. Such men, standing out on the platform of an east-bound caboose, or an observation car, was the way we made heroes, out here, before Babe Ruth came along. We made our dream of fair-women through the Diner windows where such a man, seated across from this woman, poured water from a crystal goblet into a crystal glass. We made our dream of the future night after night as the Flyer passed, trailing the wild whistle, and the stream of coaches, full of such men and women, made a band of light across the wide plain. But the times have changed. We try to make things differently now.

We've given up, I know, trying to make men of small boys that way. I think we've also given up the notion that it can be done. I used to laugh at my father when he said that he voted for William Jennings Bryan because he wanted a man, as well as a monkey, for President. Back then it was men out of monkeys, now it's monkeys out of men. Men are born and raised, my father said, other people are educated—and by that he meant to dismiss my notions, as well as himself. In his opinion we had both lost an essential thing. Men of that caliber produced, it would seem, everything in the world but men of that caliber—out of a silk purse it is also hard to make a good sow's ear.

Now when my father sat here a good many men walked the ties. Not far, perhaps, but they set off walking on them.

The man who knew about that was a friend of my father's, and at some time or other he must have told him his story, as my father began it, I know, time after time. He called it Tom Scanlon's story—but he never finished it.

"Tom Scanlon—" my father would say, then, as he was a man who never smoked, take a match from his vest and put it in the corner of his mouth. If you were standing at that point, you would sit down. My father would swing his chair around and point through the window, toward the cattle loader, but just to the left—at the rear of the New Western Hotel. Tom Scanlon had a room on the top floor, facing the west.

The Western Hotel was built at a time when men were saying, "go west, young man, go west—" but the town of Junction, as well as all the young men, was going east. No house or store, no building of any kind, lay to the west. The windows on the west side of the hotel looked out on a spur of the main line tracks, several piles of tarred ties, and a mile or so of burned ditch grass. In the winter and early spring this grass was green, a fresh, winter-wheat color, but people in the hotel always had the burned smell in their noses. As there was a prevailing western wind the smell of the grass hung over the town, and never left the rooms, Tom Scanlon said, of the Western Hotel. In the middle of the winter a man could smell it in the hall. City women would sometimes wake their husbands, sure that there was a fire in the building, or throw up the windows and look out in the street, or the empty side yard. In the early summer a Carnival might be there. And in the early morning, a little after sunrise, a man might see as far as Chapman, where the sun would be bright on the tin roof of the grain elevator. The wide plain would be green, like a sea of grass, winter wheat, or whatever you want to call it, with a house here and there at the end of a sand-colored road. One could see by the tracks, crossing and recrossing, tangled on themselves like so many mop strings, that neither the traffic, nor the road, were going anywhere. What traffic there was went to the east. As the afternoon sun was hot on the windows, fading the bedspreads and the rug on the floor, the woman who made the beds made it a point to draw the blinds. Very few men ever troubled to let them up. They were all traveling men, and they knew well enough what the view was. Newcomers, however, Omaha people who didn't know grass from winter wheat, would sometimes raise the blind and stand there and look out. They would see the plain, the dark tracks in the road, and if the last snow had melted they would see the charred fence posts from last summer's fires. The chances are they would not raise the blind on that side again.

The front of the Hotel was on Main street, where there were wide steps, and a hitching bar, but men like Tom Scanlon hardly ever came in that way. At some time or other some traveling man—very likely just one man to start with—got into the habit of coming in the rear. The back door was right there, facing the tracks, with a night lantern above it, and saved a tired man the walk around to the front. They were traveling men, and anxious to get to bed. Over a period of time what one man started—Tom Scanlon, in my father's opinion—became the general rule for traveling men. They came in through the back, two or three at a time, stopped long enough to see what was cooking, then dropped their bags in the lobby and went upstairs. They gave up, more or less, signing the ledger, and some of the more regular men kept their keys in their pocket, not troubling to turn them in. It saved everybody quite a bit of needless work. There was no fuss and bother, everybody knew where everything was. The old timers paid their bills when they thought of it. They left their sample bags in the lobby, their hats on the back of the chairs, and fell into the habit of treating the place like home.

This fellow Tom Scanlon, for instance, was known to have slept in his clothes. He smoked a good deal, lying in bed, and left his cigars in a pile in the nightpot, which he kept on the chair at the side of his bed. When he got sleepy he would pull the quilt over his legs. Even in winter he seldom got between the sheets. An odd man, in many ways, he liked the small room at the back where the only window opened on the west. Right straight down the tracks, the telephone poles, and the semaphores. Sometimes Mrs. Riddlemosher would find him sitting there. There was no excuse for this as there were comfortable chairs in the lobby, a brass rail for your feet, and a big window on the street. But in the winter, when it got dark early, Tom Scanlon was known to pull his bed, lazy as he was, over to the window so he could look out. Men walking down the tracks would see the glow of his cigar.

Over the years Tom Scanlon saw a good many things, where, as a rule, there was nothing to see, the next crossing being clear out of town. Just for that reason men would use it now and then. Maybe to go around a freight, that had stopped on the siding, or to do away with the nuisance of the railway gates. Waiting for those poles to go up or down irritated some men. They would drive their teams west, to the open crossing, and every now and then, two or three times a year, number 7, with the east-bound mail, would meet them there. Sometimes, it was said, the wind was strong, blowing from the east against the whistle, and sometimes, so it seemed, the man just didn't give a damn. Anyhow, that was what my father said. Around the turn of the century a good many men seemed to feel that way. Sometimes Tom Scanlon would see the team standing there, their traces dragging, as if they had walked off and left the buggy on the farm. Or he might see the buggy, and have to look around for the team. Now and then he saw a horse tossed up in the air, like a bale of hay, with the driver left sitting, or standing, with the reins in his hands. Or his hands there, firmly clasped, but the reins gone. And for reasons of their own all kinds of men, with a bottle in their hand and one in their stomach, figured there was no finer place in the world to walk than the ties. Right down the center, right down the middle, to Kingdom Come. Men who didn't seem to give—as my father said—a good goddam.

Try to explain what it was they liked about the tracks? What it was they saw, far down at the end, while walking the ties. Men in their teens, with a soft red beard, or men in their forties, with everything to live for, or men without it, but for the moment with a bottle in their hand. Anyhow, they saw something. Tom Scanlon insisted on that. And he would have been the man to know as he saw these men, wandering out in the evening, stopping now and then to lift the bottle, or hold it to the light. Seeing in the bottle, as the saying goes, what they seemed to see on the horizon, where the tracks pointed toward the red and green lights, the swinging semaphores. Tom Scanlon was the only man in town who knew that the place to look for Emil Bickel was not in Omaha, or Kansas City, but on the telephone wires. There he swung, like a sack of grain, his arms dangling like the sleeves of a scarecrow, and every last button gone from his vest. Popped, so my father said, by the force of it. A good man, with an honest wife, three sturdy kids. There was a freight parked on the siding and some men said that Emil Bickel, a man with everything to live for, had stepped out from behind it, died that way. Other men said that was just a way of leaving town. Of getting away, so to speak, from what you had on your mind. The only man who might have known was Tom Scanlon, but all he ever said, at that time or later, was where they should look for him. Emil Bickel had been dressed for church, and the watch in his pocket, the crystal unbroken, had stopped at exactly eleven-seventeen. The night mail, rolling down the grade, had been ninety seconds late.

No, no doubt about it, Tom Scanlon had seen a good many things. Sitting there at the window, leaving burns on the sill with his cigars. No one would have said, however, that was why he was lying there. A man named Muncy once suggested that Tom Scanlon, as everybody knew, spent his time in bed because he was just too damn lazy to walk. Or he would have been killed, like a lot of other men, along the tracks himself. Not that he was a drinker, but he certainly didn't give a hoot. When he died in bed, a cigar in his mouth, a good many men would have felt cheated—except for the fact that he sat the night pot on his head. Very likely he knew it, when it came, but as he didn't have the time to walk out on the tracks, and to die like a man, he did what he could. He took the nightpot and sat it on his head. It had been full of his stubbed cigars, and they lay all around him, spilled into his lap, and left a grey, hoarfrost ash in his dark beard. And yet not a ghoulish sight at all, as the woman who had found him said, but very much like him, another one of his pranks so to speak. So much so, so exactly like him, that she stood in the door, wagging her finger, thinking that he was making another prank for her. She wasn't really sure until she saw that his cigar, a King Edward, was out.

"Oh there—Muncy!"

In the window I faced, where I had wiped a spot clean, I could see the old man with the bandy legs coming down the tracks. He held several yellow papers in his right hand. Coming up he said, "Pete back there told me he'd seen you walkin' down the tracks. Told me he told you nobody from here walked the ties like that." He grinned. "I just told him your Daddy walked 'em all the time. I guess a lot of us did." He held the papers up and said, "Occurred to me you might like to have your Daddy's papers, ones he wrote himself, no good to me anymore." He held out one sheet, an old Western Union blank (my father always kept a pad along with him for letters), and on this he had written in his stiff, telegraphic hand, a minimum of pronouns and adjectives.

TELEGRAPH ANY SALT LAKE BANK FIFTY
DIRECT WAIVING IDENTIFICATION.

"Honeymoon—" he said, "guess they stopped to see the

Temple. What's the date on there?"

"Nineteen-four," I said.

"More'n forty years—reason we still got it your Daddy always wrote in indelible pencil." The capital letters—where he moistened the pencil point—were still dark. It was signed Will Muncy, and could be read, as I knew without looking, on both sides of the paper.

"Well, many thanks," I said.

"I thought you might like to have them," he said. He puffed sharply on his own cigar, and though mine was out I broke out in a sweat. I tossed mine away, across the tracks, and wiped my face with my sleeve. The other side of my father, the man of few words but the long rhetorical dreams, the man who believed in the formula, the man who went to Chicago on a railroad pass, to stand in the lobby of the Drake Hotel while the red-capped boys paged Will Clayton Muncy in the dining room. My father, too, suffered from home-town nausea. Perhaps that feeling at the pit of the stomach that I felt now, and an hour ago, was common to the men who walked right down the middle of the tracks. To Tom Scanlon, among them, who showed the range and power of this feeling by lifting a nightpot and setting it on his head. And my father, who used his railroad passes to find a city girl, a pretty hula dancer, in order to shock—as he said—the living daylights out of them.

"There's folks who don't care for these things," he went on, and put the rest in my hand, his own hand along with them, "but your missus said you'd be glad to have anything. She said you never talked much about your Daddy, what he was like."

"Well, I suppose that's true," I said.

"She said she was well up on Grace—that's your mother —an' Grace's folks, especially old man Osborn, but that your Daddy was pretty much in cog-nee-toe." He paused, "That's the way your Daddy was quite a bit." He nodded at the window. "Sittin' in there, in cog-nee-toe."

"Well, I guess I better get back," I said, "or I'll be in cog-nee-toe myself."

He shook his head. "There's no rush. She told me to tell you that." I looked at him and he said, "Think Mabel knew your Daddy. Yes, think she did. Guess she an' the missus got quite a bit to talk about." He turned away— "You find you got time you might drop by the bank, white door on the side. Think I might turn up another note or two before you get away."

"The truth is—" I said, "Dad wasn't much for writing letters. I don't suppose I've got, right now, more than a note or two."

"Well, I'll take a peek around." He grinned—"Give me something to do." He walked back from where he had come, not on the ties but in the loose cinders, stopping below the gates to shade his eyes, talk to the man in the tower. They watched me go along the tracks toward the Western Hotel. The last time I saw Bud Hibbard he lived in a house behind the hotel, a two-acre farm with a garage and a place for chickens to run. The chickens, more than likely, would still be there.

My father said that Junction got its name when the C. B. & Q., running north and south, crossed the main line of the Union Pacific just a quarter mile east of the square. But the town had never made up its mind which line to parallel. Half the roads came into town at odd angles, and people living in the C. B. & Q. part of Junction always felt like strangers when they crossed the main line. As a boy, I was apt to get lost now and then. But I never saw the problem for what it was until Bud Hibbard, the third year of the war, took me aside to tell me that the end of the world was at hand. Naturally, we wanted a view of something like that. We went up the ladder in the Hibbard elevator until we could see, as from a ferris wheel, the island of Junction in the wide sea of corn. The world didn't end, as I remember, but I saw how it was that the Hibbards faced the West, while the Muncys, and the rest of the town, looked to the East. Our compasses had been set differently. For reasons not at all clear to me my friend Bud Hibbard, with the new world before him, turned his back on it and moved into a house facing the tracks. Perhaps Clinton Hibbard had had something to do with it. A man who drove a Franklin with an air-cooled engine, and who went clear to Indiana, and the deep south, to find himself a woman fit to ride in it. A tall, thin woman who drove herself around in a buggy-wheeled electric, making a humming sound like the telephone wires running along the tracks. When Clinton Hibbard built this woman a home, in the manner to which she was accustomed, he took a city block and built it where he thought the new town would soon be. A house with seventeen rooms, every room with great windows rising from the floor to nearly the ceiling, and pieces of Indiana flagstone set into the yard for a walk. When it was clear that this woman, this Miss Caddy, was not going to fill even one room with children, Aunt Angeline and Uncle

Billie Hibbard, the old folks, moved in to live with them. That's how it was, that's where things stood, when I was a boy. Aunt Angie spent most of her time in the kitchen, and the year I left, early in the spring, a room was added to the kitchen to take care of Uncle Billie and his drying seeds. A silent old man, with a box of strong snuff on the arm of his chair, or on the floor beside him, he more or less lived in the garden he could see from his bed. Ears of drying seed corn hung from the rafters, and around the walls. The old man seldom talked, as it might cost him a swallow of juice, or a thick quid of snuff, which sometimes dried on the bib of his overalls while he was asleep.

At the front of the house there was always a party, young men who rented teams to drive down from Lincoln, and young women who stayed all night rather than risk breathing the night air. Crossing the damp lawn with a handkerchief held to their nose.

Did this go on forever? I'm afraid I thought it did. *When I was a boy* is just a way of saying that though other things change, and though another time passes, these things are like the castle in the ball of clear glass on the sewing machine. They are there forever. They will spring to life if we so much as handle them.

Bud Hibbard's house was a square box with a peaked roof, on a concrete platform—quite a bit the worse for wear but still where I had left it in my glass ball.

A lilac bush at the front, to the left of the porch, and in the center of the yard a truck tire, painted white, sprouting a single hollyhock like a leaky fire hose. At the back of the house the same garage, but a lean-to shed had been added, and through the high chicken wire I could see the leghorn pullets—and they could see me. A few rows of sweet corn marked the garden, and through the open door to the garage I could see a cultivator, with a gasoline motor, and sacks of laying mash. There was a view, of a kind, to the rear, or rather there would be in the evening when the curtain of heat, like the air over hot ashes, stopped blurring the land. Then there would be a hollow, with two dead trees, and beyond the trees the circling shell pattern where Swenson's cows made their way around the green slope. One of the Swenson boys, little Eric, would be waiting in the hollow, with a short length of rope, and he would run the lead cow till her tail was up like a whip tassel. It would all be there, pretty much as I had left it, and I would have been willing to settle for that if I hadn't, somehow or other, overlooked something.

The woman. The woman standing at the screen. I would know this woman, when I met her, as *the finest living creature on God's green earth*—but as yet I didn't know her. There was still some chance for me. I looked at my watch—a man without a watch dies two deaths for every man that has one—then I turned, watch in hand, and nearly trampled a small boy.

"Whoopsa-daisy," I said, and scooped him up—he was wearing an inflated red rubber inner tube, a man's painter's hat, and that's about all. When I set him on his feet he backed off to look at me. A little towhead, with light blue eyes. It suddenly occurred to me that he was the first, and the only boy, that I had seen. Where were the kids? Were they across the tracks in the brave new world?

"Well son—" I began——

"You the man that knows my Daddy?" he said. He

lowered the tube to scratch at a spot on his seat. Times change, no doubt about it, but if this towheaded boy was a Hibbard——

"What's your name, son?" I said.

"Steve—" he said. "What's yours?"

"My name is Muncy," I said, "what's your Daddy's name?"

"My father's name is Mister Hibbard," he said, and now that we were acquainted he dropped the inner tube, looked at his belly button. It was one of the kind that stuck out—he pushed it in. "My father's name is Mister Hibbard, my mother's name is Mrs. Hibbard, and my little sister's name is Angeline Hibbard. Mine is Steve."

"Those are fine names," I said, "that's just fine." I put my hand in my pocket—something I owe to my early life with my father—and took out a handful of small change.

"My mother's waving at you," he said. "Aren't you going to wave at her?"

I turned, the loose change in one hand, the other prepared to wave, and saw Mrs. Hibbard, the screen ajar, beckoning to me.

"My mother's other name is Nellie," the boy said, and gathered up the inner tube, like a life belt, and walked ahead of me across the yard.

In her arms Nellie Hibbard held a baby which she shifted to her hip, saddle fashion, in order to wipe the loose bib of her apron across her face. A little woman, around five feet, she had the pronounced dishwater pallor of women who breathe the open air, but never get into it. Wisps of mousy hair, neither light nor dark, were streaked on her damp forehead, the rest were done up in wire curlers, like small sausages. Her eyes were pale, but direct, with that glint of humor people have who recognize it as a last resort.

"I suppose Stevie's told you all about us—" she said.

"Well, I know you're Mrs. Hibbard," I said, "and he knows I'm Mr. Muncy."

"First Mrs. Criley called—" she said. "Mr. Criley, Leo, is at the bank—then less than ten minutes ago Bud called himself. He said there was a city man in town, so it must be you. He said you was the only one who would get out and fuss around."

"News certainly gets around, doesn't it?" I said.

"It's not so bad as it sounds," Nellie said. "You see Bud's at the switchboard, and now with the strike on he's there all alone. He can't help hearing about what's going on. When he heard you were out on west Pioneer he knew it was you."

"Well, I'm very glad to meet you, Mrs. Hibbard—" I said.

"He said if it was you not to let you get away. He said he'd never forgive me if I let you get out of this house." As she opened the screen she said, "I understand you're a family man, Mr. Muncy?"

"I guess so," I said, "we've got two of them."

"Well, that's a family as far as I'm concerned," she said.

She said that in such a manner that I gathered that it wasn't—not by a long shot—considered a family where she came from. I was facing the piano, and a framed picture that included a bearded man, a large woman, and nine or ten children gathered around them, affectionately. When I turned back to her, she said—"You people ever wonder how they managed?" She looked around the room. "It seems I'm always ashamed about how things look."

"We know how that is," I said. "We've had to raise both of them in one small room."

"I don't see how you did it." She put the little one down, then bent over to see if she was wet. "I've read about that," she said, "but you can't believe everything you read."

"No indeed," I said.

She stepped behind me to hook the screen, then she had to unhook it to let in the boy. "First he wants in, then he wants out, and if it isn't him it's the fool dog." Somewhere in the house I heard the dog's tail thump, then stop. "I feel as if I know you people," she said, "Bud's talked about you so much." She turned to the boy. "If you're going to make that noise you can just go out." He was letting the air out of the inner tube. He held the valve in his mouth, waiting for the bubbles to appear. "I suppose it's just you we've talked about," she said, "as I don't think Bud ever met the missus. I don't think Bud thought of you as a family man."

"Neither does my wife," I said, but she didn't smile. It's hard to say just where people are different, but Nellie Hibbard still had the notion that the place to look for a man was in his face. Not at his tie, nor his shoes, except to see that they properly fit him, and were not outlandish in the manner of a foreigner. And she seemed to find it natural that I should look at her.

The finest of God's living creatures—as she would always be to the man who knew her—might have struck you differently when you passed her in the dime store, or out

[54]

on the street. First of all, you might not have noticed her. Unless she asked you to hold the little one while she found the change in her purse. Nellie Hibbard had the stance, the posture, of a woman who lives facing the sink, the abdomen forward, pressing against it, the shoulders drooped. In a sun-tired land, full of too much light, her face and arms had the color of a change-maker on the Seventh Avenue subway. She turned to take the valve from the boy's mouth, and in the house, quiet now, I could hear the applause of some radio program. The applause stopped, and a man's voice said—"Ladies——"

"Is the missus somewhere you can call her?" Nellie said. "Or you want me to call Bud. He can just as well go by an' pick her up."

"I'd better let her know," I said. "Is there a phone at Mabel's Lunch?"

"2–4–9," said Nellie, "but the phone's out here. You want to come out here?" I followed her to the kitchen. The radio was on a shelf over the sink. As I picked up the phone, she reached up, as if for a light cord, and tuned it down. The phone was on the dresser beside the sink.

"I'll get it for you," Nellie said, and putting the phone to her ear, said, "Honey, give me Mabel 2–4–9." As it buzzed she passed the receiver to me.

"Mabel's Lunch," said the voice.

"This is Mr. Muncy," I said, "could you tell me if my wife, Mrs. Muncy, is there?"

"Clyde Muncy," she said, "we've been waitin' for you to call." When I didn't answer she said, "This is Mabel, don't you remember?"

"Hello Mabel," I said.

"Well, we've been wonderin' where you were."

"I'm out here at Mr. Hibbard's, Bud Hibbard—" I said, "and I wonder if you would tell my wife how to get out here, Mrs. Hibbard would like to meet her."

"Your wife's out in your car," she said, "but your little girl is right here."

"Tell her her Daddy would like to speak to her." Mabel put the phone down, and I heard her say, "That's him all right. I knew it was him." Then she said, "Come here honey, this is your Daddy on the phone."

"Hello Daddy——"

"This is your father—" I said. "Where is Mummy?"

"She doesn't want to talk to you. Not one word."

"Tell your mother," I said, "that Mr. Hibbard, your Daddy's old friend, has asked him to stay right here until he gets home."

"You know what she'll say to that?"

"Never mind," I said, "you tell her."

"He'll be just sick," Nellie said, "if you folks don't stay for supper."

"Tell your mother," I said, "that Mrs. Hibbard insists that we stay for supper. That she wants to meet the family. Tell your mother that."

"Hmmmmm—" the girl said. It was her mother's voice.

"Tell her to drive one block east then right straight down to the end of the street. The last house. The one at the end of the street."

"Here comes Mummy now," she said.

"You tell her," I said, and hung up. I stood there with the phone in my hand.

"Is she coming?" Nellie said. Before I could answer the phone rang. "That's Bud—you take it," she said.

[56]

"Hello—" I said.

"Hello—" the voice said—"that you?"

"This is Clyde Muncy," I said, "that you Bud?" No answer. "Is that you Bud?" I said.

"I can hardly get it out," the voice said. "That you Clyde?"

"This is me," I said.

"Holy smoke, Clyde," he said. "Holy mackerel, think of that."

"If you're thinking of coming by," I said, "you might drop by Mabel and pick up my wife. You know how women are."

"I know," he said, soberly. "I'll drive right by."

"We've got a Ford, 35—" I said. "Two kids in the back."

"Holy Mackerel, Clyde—" he said, "you comin' back?"

"I wouldn't say that," I said, "we're just passing through." No answer to that.

"Hello Bud—" I said, "you still there?"

"Right here," he said.

"Well Bud," I said, "I really think you better have a look at my wife. Pretty quick. She might drive off and leave me here."

"I'm going right by, Clyde," he said, "is Nellie there? Let me speak to Nellie."

I gave her the phone.

"This me, Bud—" she said, then—"say you pick up some corn. You're always tellin' me how the two of you used to eat corn." Then she put back the receiver, without any comment, and lifted the baby to the sink board. Absently, she passed her left hand over her hip. It was wet, the print of flowers looked bright and fresh. "Well,

[57]

sweetie pie—" she said, and rolled the little one over on her back. "You want to hold her, Clyde—" she said, and I put my hand on her tummy, slippery with talcum powder, while Nellie went out in the back yard. Through the sink window, over the line of wash, I watched her file the clothes pins in her mouth as she took down the diapers, folded them over her arm.

One trouble with my wife that sometimes fills me with admiration, other times with self pity, is that sensible people wonder why she married me. They recognize a better human being, immediately. I accept this judgment in the same way that I acknowledge the premises on which it is made—my wife gives, without thinking about it, more of herself. She is capable, so to speak, of loving something. There are other factors, but the one that men and women recognize, and know to be holy, is this naive generosity with one's self. Without calculation, therefore without malice, profit, or loss. Not that that is why I married her. That was long, long ago, at a time that I doubted I would ever meet a better person than myself, and if I had, I would have had more sense than marry her. But it may help to explain why she married me. Women have a place in their heart for men who are buoyed up with such a notion, think well of their talents, and believe they have the world by the tail. They feel for this man a great pity, understandably. And then time passes, and if the man is such a fool as to persist in these notions, this pity may give way to admiration, even to love. This woman may accept the man's notions for her own. Not really, but in good facsimile.

Through the window I could see that Bud Hibbard recognized this. He leaned on the running-board of our car, smiling at the kids, talking to my wife, and wondering how it came about that such a woman married me. He was still a little man, on the wiry side, with clothes that still seemed too small for him, but he was better looking than I remembered him. When we were kids his black hair seemed to grow right out of his eyes. Now he had a forehead, a rather good one, and still plenty of hair. Nellie, her arms full of diapers, stood at his side. I might say that I do find it trying when the wives of my friends, as well as my friends, show an obvious preference for my wife. I raised the curtain, put out my head, and called—"Don't forget I'm the one you came home to see," and watched Bud lean back from the car, start across the yard. As he stepped to the porch I noticed the patch of gray hair along his temples, and the salt-and-pepper glint in his day-old beard. I had to wait until then—that moment—to know that time had passed.

"Well, you look about the same—" Bud said, and turned from the sink, the towel in his hands, as if he saw an early picture of me on the opposite wall. "He look like you think he'd look, Nellie?" he said.

"I don't know," said Nellie. "Think he looks quite a bit like anybody else."

We were standing in a room about the size of a freight elevator, in a store like Wanamakers, surrounded by furniture on its way from the basement to the customer. The bargain basement, where $99.50 would once furnish a five-room house, every room in the new and wonderful *waterfall* veneer. As Bud's house only had four rooms some of the overflow was in the kitchen, the dining room table, and the waterfall dresser with the drawer knobs removed. Over my wife's head, nodding as she talked to Nellie, I could see the LONE WOLF under the same winter sky, preserved, as in amber, behind two sheets of glass. He looked less wolf-like to me now, but not at all bored. In the valley full of lamplight was home-sweet-home, a new fall of snow on the roof and chimney, and the never-ending problem of what the Lone Wolf intended to do. I didn't know then. It was clear that I didn't know now. As I always do when faced with a stickler I turned my head.

On the piano behind me, along with Nellie's family, were photographs of the boy with hand-painted blue eyes, and a photograph of Nellie and Bud, with their first-born in his arms. The dog Skeezix was also in the picture, but a little blurred. The room we stood in had the look of Nellie in the photograph. Nellie dressed for town—red hat and shoes, a beaded white bag, a real butterfly pin, and a dark blue suit freely sprinkled with hair, bits of string and diaper lint. A settled crease at the front of the skirt like the wrinkle at the front of the rug.

On the red plush chairs, and on the davenport—the seat too high with the day-bed beneath it—papers were spread to keep off the dog, and the family. To keep off Steve, inside again, with his inner tube dripping water, and to keep off Angeline, now that she was beginning to crawl. And perhaps the old man, until he had washed, got his pants changed. Some people might say that this room looked a good deal like the people in it—perhaps it did in the sense that it looked like all of us. It looked like the difference between our fathers and ourselves. This difference is the measure we have taken of the new world, and made it ours, or it is the measure of the extent that we have failed. This house, Bud Hibbard's house, had failed. What could be said—that somehow we all had slipped the moment we took our first step forward, the moment we reached, with both hands, for the better world? For the living room suit—as my father called it—with red plush cushions on every chair, and on the floor not a rug to walk on, but a rug to match. Blue once, now the color of diaper lint. I looked down the front of my Wanamaker pants at my Florsheim shoes, on the better world rug, offered at a great saving by Sears, Roebuck & Co. The room was small, we stood huddled together, but my wife's voice seemed a little high as she described how fond she was of red and blue. That was, until the children came along. When they came along, why we just had to give up the rug. Was there anything in the world, she said, made to show up a piece of lint, or the drag of a diaper, like one of those blue broadloom rugs?

That was the God's truth, Nellie said, but when you pay forty-three dollars for a rug, blue or white, there was nothing left to do but wear it out. She bent over, her knees pressed together, to pick up a length of string, a wad of cat hair, several bobby pins, and a small hard cake of chicken dung. In the quiet we could hear the hissing tube around Steve's waist, and a certain excitement, I thought, among the hens. I cleared my throat, but didn't say anything. I had the feeling that to be heard I would have to raise my voice—as a man leans forward out of a plush rocking-chair.

"You men going to stand there," Nellie said, "or you going to see what's into those chickens?"

"You got two kids, or one, Clyde?" Bud said.

"Two—" I said, looking around.

"Well—" said Bud, "I guess one of them's in the chicken house."

He walked out of the room and I followed him. As we crossed the room the radio, like a friendly voice in the window, cautioned me to think twice about baby's soap. Asked me if I knew why baby had such a precious skin. The radio was on the shelf, over the sink, the tuning knob caked with flour, soap powder and a piece of black jack gum. As we passed the sink Bud reached out and switched it off. At the back door he turned to see if that caught my eye. It had.

"They turn it on and just let it run." He shook his head.

"I know—" I said.

"You ask them what they're listenin' to and they won't know, half the time. Just the noise. I suppose it's like someone around the house."

"Sure—" I said. We left the house and walked out in the back yard. The grass in the yard grew in clumps, like broom ends, and between each clump the earth was packed down hard, honed smooth with barefeet. There were mulberry stains on the tire swing, and Bud stepped out of his way to give it a twist, rattle the marbles left inside.

As we reached the hen house he said, "Might be a black snake, we have 'em—but more than likely one of your kids." He slipped the latch from the door and we peered into the corners, saw nothing. The smell was strong, and I couldn't picture *my* girl sitting in there. Just a week ago, on her Granddaddy's farm, she had discovered that *Moo* in a barn was a good deal different than *Mooo* in a book.

"Let me switch on the light," Bud said, but before he reached the switch a voice said—

"Now don't get upset—here I am."

The light came on and there she was, back on the roost. She was squatting on a piece of newspaper she had remembered to bring along.

"Well, explain yourself," I said.

"I just wanted to see—" she said, "how they did it."

"Did what?" I said.

"Roosted—" she said. "What do you think?"

"Isn't that a city kid for you?" Bud said.

"If your mother saw you—" I began, then turned to look at Bud. "A city kid—" I said, "just what do you mean by that?"

"Who else but a city kid would ever think of doing that?" Bud said. He wagged his head. "That's a city kid all right."

"I've done a good deal worse than sit in with a bunch of hens," I said, "and maybe you can remember that I wasn't a city kid."

Bud thought about that. "Well, you were different anyway. Ask anybody in town, they'll all tell you that."

"If I wanted to know something," I said, "the last person I would ask is anyone in this town. Why city kid —since I'm so different, maybe she gets all of this from me?"

"Well, there's that too—" said Bud.

"Just what does this all add up to?" I said.

"All I'm saying is—" Bud said, "that only a city kid would go sit on a roost." He wagged his head. "A girl too. What kind of girl would do something like that?"

"Speaking of country kids," I said, "if I remember correctly I was born in Lone Tree—weren't you born in Omaha?"

"We were there for seventeen months," said Bud.

"Just what I thought," I said, "a city boy." I leaned over, at that point, and spit in the yard. "Let me tell you something, Bud—" I said, "if you'd like to be popular with my wife don't mention this city-boy stuff while she's around. Before you get around to that subject you better put that radio down in the basement, and send that city-furniture back to Monkey Ward."

"Why the devil you people so touchy?" Bud said.

"When you bring that boy of yours to New York," I said, "I'll try to see him for what he is. I'm not going to take out a label, lettered HICK, and paste it on him. I'll even try to overlook the fact that his Daddy was born in Omaha, a mighty big town with candy machines on the theatre seats."

"You people talk like that before your children?" said Bud.

"Where we come from," I said, "there isn't much room. There isn't room to do our talking behind their backs." We stood there, and my city-kid walked away.

"I'm sorry, Bud—" I said. "I don't mean that. We both respect the fact that you don't talk like that—but you make it pretty hard with this city-kid stuff. Suppose we start over. Suppose we drop this labelling."

[64]

"If I'd just known you was so touchy, Clyde—" he said.

"Don't say it!" I said. He didn't. "Let me put it this way," I said, "my kid has been out here five days, your kid was born and raised out here. Suppose we ask your kid where the chickie's egg comes from?"

"Why, he takes it for granted," said Bud.

"Good—" I said. "My kids don't. Suppose we just call them my kids from now on——o-kay?"

"You know—" said Bud, closing the hen house door, "You're the same old Clyde."

The Hibbard place was about two acres, with one given over to gardening, and we walked through the garden to the fence at the rear. His neighbor's water tank sat at the turn of the fence. I had heard so much talk, in the last twenty years, of the dreary flatness of Nebraska, that I had come to think of it as flat myself. Perhaps I had never known the land could be beautiful.

"You ever see—" Bud said, propping his foot on the fence rail, "anything any prettier than that?"

Well, maybe I had. But I wasn't sure. I had seen country like that in France, but that was long ago, I was an exile, and I thought it was France—in country like that —that appealed to me. I would say that Bud Hibbard would feel right at home in a French provincial town, once he got over the notion that berets were rather strange hats. A Protestant Yankee at home in Catholic France. I remember a French funeral I once saw, moving down a white road in Cézanne's country, and the only thing I felt to be missing was a Model T Ford. The white dust rising from the narrow bicycle tires. The old man's gaze straight ahead, his hands vibrating on the wheel. That painting of Cézanne, the card players, could hang on the wall behind the coke burner, between the calendars, and nobody would find it strange. After all is said and done, or dead and buried, or hashed up and warmed over, the land is the potter and where it shows its hand men are the same. On other frontiers, right now, were the young men who entered Nebraska, with the same dream, just eighty years ago. That dream was young. Was ours growing old? Had we found replacements for these parts of our life? Or had we been victimized by the fact that abstinence, frugality, independence were not the seeds of heroes, but the roots of the great soft life. Out of frugality—in this rich land—what could come but abundance, and out of abundance different notions of a brave new world. For every man—as we now say—a full dinner pail. Another way to say that—the one I heard from my father, and perhaps you heard it from your father—"I don't want my son to have to go through what I went through." What was that? What made men of them? What made *that* kind of man, anyhow, and perhaps there was more than a casual connection between that kind of man and what we call our way of life. It was his. He had earned it. Can you give such a life to anyone?

Turning from the water tank Bud said, "I'm so sick and tired of these strikes. You have strikes where you come from?"

"Strikes—?" I said. "You have strikes out here?"

"I'm doing the work of five men," he said, "—they tell me I am." I waited, and he said, "The funny thing about it is that I can do it. A man who will work is worth the whole dang lot of them."

[66]

"Who are they?" I said. "City people?"

"I know what you're thinking, but that's who they are. Some of them live in Lincoln. One or two keep their families in Omaha."

"What are they paid?"

"More than they're worth. I'm paid eighty-five cents an hour. There isn't a one of them who isn't paid more than me."

"This the outfit," I said, "you've been with for fifteen years?"

"You're thinking—why don't I ask for a raise myself? Well, I'll tell you. For what I'm doing I'm paid well enough. Anybody can do it. It's not worth more than sixty cents an hour."

"But *anybody* can't live on that, Bud—" I said. "Whatever it's worth a man has to live on it."

"Clyde, you're wrong. You can't pay a man more than he's worth. If you start doing that, where you going to stop? We're living on eighty cents an hour. Some of these guys claim they can't live on two dollars. I've heard of people who can't live on fifty thousand a year. When you talk like that where you going to stop?" He raised his hand to his face and said, "We got kids in the office, Clyde, who do nothing all day but talk about a 'living wage.' I never heard a one of them mention their work. When I talk about mine they grin at me. They think I'm a sap. They don't say so, but that's what they think. Wherever these kids come from, Clyde, they've been told that the Company is against them, and that what they have to do is be against the Company. Well, the Company feeds them. Without it every last one of them would starve to death."

"I've heard that put the other way—" I said.

"I suppose you've heard that the world owes them a living?"

"Yes, I've heard that."

"Well, you know Clyde, they're right. If they're ever going to get a living, these kids, the world owes it to them. There isn't a damn one of them that could earn an honest red cent. The only thing they really want is that check in the mail to be more this time than it was the last time, and to have managed to have done even less for it. They've got a fine program. Can any man see the end of that?"

"There's people like that in Junction?" I said.

"They weren't born here, Clyde—but any day now they will be. They're turning them out like hot rolls in those cabins across the tracks."

"Like city-kids?" I said, but the irony let me down. I didn't feel it. I didn't smile when he looked up.

"That's the God's truth, Clyde—" he said, and slapped his fist down on the rail. "I'll tell you I don't see where we're going anymore. They all think the Company is the bitch and all they have to do is lie and tug at her udders. You can't wean them. They like it as it is. They don't want to grow up."

"You talk like this before your children?" I said.

He didn't smile, "Bygolly Clyde, some day I'm just afraid that I will." He looked at me, then said, "You know, Clyde, we're going in the red."

"You are—?" I said.

"Me—" he said. "The Company." Then he said, "You're laughing?"

"No, I'm not laughing."

"You remember how he put it?"

"He who?" I said.

"Old Abe—" he said, "you remember how he put it? He said he didn't go into it for this, or for that. He said he went into it to save the Union."

"The Company?" I said.

"That's my cut of the Union. We support the Union, the Union supports us."

"Well, you haven't changed much either," I said.

"I don't know what we're coming to," said Bud. "It gives me a funny feeling at times."

"Well, that's a city feeling," I said. "Now you know something else about city people. They lie awake, some of them, feeling it."

"So do I," said Bud. I could see that he did.

"Well, I didn't drive back here," I said, "to talk about how we feel in the city. What's new or old—anybody I might know?"

We turned from the fence and started toward the house.

"You remember Emory?" I nodded. "He's singing on the radio. Some people seem to like it. Guess they pay him for it, anyway."

"You ever hear of Pauline?"

"Last time I heard," he said, stooping for a tomato, "she was working in a dime store in Omaha."

"The first thing to turn green in the spring—" I said, "is the Christmas jewelry—"

"What made you think of that?"

"Damned if I know."

"Well—" he said, "I suppose it's true enough." He

picked three more tomatoes and we started toward the house. My boy was sitting in the tire swing—*his* boy pushing him. That was city-kid stuff too, but I didn't mention it.

"Say—" Bud said, "I nearly forgot. You remember Orville?"

Yes, I did. I remembered him pretty well. An odd boy who sat at the back of the room as the other seats were too small for him, playing with an assortment of objects he found in the lining of his pants. He invented shocking machines, lewd stories, a machine for throwing your voice, and held the opinion that most murderers had an extra small toe.

"What about him?" I said.

"He's doing some writing. He's got a new book out right now."

"So—?" I said.

"I got it downstairs," said Bud, "if you'd like to take a look at it." He opened the screen and we stepped inside. The radio was back on and above the voice of a man, singing, the sound of running water and Nellie's report. The price of food. Was it ever going to stop?

"Down here—" said Bud, and we ducked down the stairs off the kitchen into the smell of sprouting potatoes, berry boxes and damp soft coal. Just thirty years ago Bud had laid claim to the room on the left, behind the furnace, and began his first plans to do something interesting with it. A den, an office, a private drafting room. Fifteen years ago, the last time I saw him, there was a large rolltop desk, several Indian baskets, and an Indian blanket on the wall. The light came on, and it looked very much the same. "One of these days—" Bud said, "I'm going to get around to fixing this up. It's really quite a place."

"You bet it is," I said.

"Could make it into an office, playroom for the kids, any number of things." He kicked a single roller-skate aside, moved a basket of Mason jars, and lifted a pile of egg cartons from the top of the desk. Under the cartons was a ledger, with a faded corduroy binding, a magnetic hammer, and a Ford carburetor on top of a book. He removed the carburetor, wiped the moon-shaped stain on his sleeve. "Here's one of them," he said, and passed the book to me.

THE SHRINKING GLOBE
How to Abate it.

There was a drawing of the globe, demonstrating the shrinkage, on the title page. Under the globe was the author's name

ORVILLE CLEVELAND ARBUTHNOT

"Was his old man really an Indian?" I said.

"Don't know—" said Bud, "but he sure looked it."

We stood there and saw, I'm sure, Mr. Arbuthnot making his rounds. He had been the mailman, in our time, a man with a dark, intense face, high cheek-bones, and the fear of God for little boys. Orville had his face, one that sometimes looked—when I turned to peer over my shoulder—like a mummy in a very fine state. The flat mouth slightly open, the nostrils like holes in his face. His mother did washing, which he delivered—summer and winter—on a wooden runner sled.

"Here's the latest one—" said Bud, and so that I might

see it better he switched on the light over my head. Large black waterbugs—those that squirt like a pinched grape when stepped on—raced their shadows, like so many marbles, across the stone floor. I stepped back. "Remember them?" said Bud.

"I think so—" I said.

"They haven't changed much either," he said. He grinned, then handed me the book.

SLEEPERS AWAKE
A Warning
of
THE IMPENDING FLOOD

The first chapter was entitled—THE CAREENING GLOBE. At the bottom of this page I read—

> Appendix outlines possibilities of postponing impending deluge by relieving pernicious mechanical pressures at source.

I looked up and said, "What's Orville doing now?"

"He's in the post office. You can see him if you want to drive by."

"I don't think we'll have the time," I said.

"He carried mail for awhile," said Bud, "but he found it made him too tired for his research."

"I can see that it would all right," I said.

"In the office he can do quite a bit of research on the job. Read his books. You ought to see the books he's got down there."

> The discovery of the careening of the globe [I read] holds the ultimate key to our salvation. Otherwise, like the hairy mammoth, we shall end up preserved in the long night of the ice.

"He has a nice prose style," I said.

"I can't say the flood worries me so much," Bud said, "but I can tell you Orville is sure a worker. Does his own research. Reads all these books himself. I've been to his room, up over the bank, and I never saw so many books in my life. Wall of books. Two three hundred books. Reads all of them himself."

"It's quite a little subject," I said.

"That's why he's doing it," said Bud. "We're all sleepers. As he says, we've got to wake up. If we don't wake up we're going to have all that ice right down on top of us."

"He ever get married?" I said.

"He went around with Mildred for awhile," said Bud. "You remember Mildred?" I nodded my head. "Then she married Leroy Kress. Lives on a farm over near Beaver Crossing. Think it was about then he got interested in this impending flood." I flipped the pages, and Bud said— "He says you and me ought to talk about this flood like people talk about the weather. That's the only way to popularize it. I know that—" said Bud, "but when it comes right down to it, I can't. I end up, every time, talking about something else."

> For over half a century [the author wound up] it has been observed that the globe is wobbling. That we are adrift on a rudderless ship, in a bottomless sea. Where is the helmsman? Who will chart our course? It is clear that the number one white man's burden is to put our globe back on its course, to provide timely arrangements for the salvation of the human race. It is up to you and me to stop the careening of our green globe.

"I don't know how you feel about the flood," said Bud,

"but I've got a lot of respect for a man who will figure something like that out for himself. Start right from scratch, with his own head, and figure it out." I remembered now, that my father had once done a book. A Mastery of the Morse Code—I think. He had learned it himself, typed it himself, and kept it in a ledger with corduroy corners in the bottom drawer on the left side of his desk. Sitting there, long winter evenings, the green shade on his eyes—he had also read it himself.

Taking the book from my hand, Bud said, "I told him you wrote too. He never heard of you either."

"There may be too many books," I said.

"Just the other day—" Bud said, "I told him, what if I'm the only man in Nebraska, the only person who ever heard of both of you?"

"What did he say?"

"I don't think he ever thought of that. Seems to me it's something you writers ought to think about." We thought about it, then he said— "There's another writer you ought to meet. Man who's proved, I guess, it wasn't this fellow Columbus after all."

"It wasn't?"

"Guess he's proved it's some fellow named Leaf, Life, or something. Says he was here first."

"Who proved this?" I said.

"Old man Swenson—wasn't he here when you were?" He turned back to the desk, rummaged in the papers at the back. "They tell me he's spent forty years of his life looking up old swords, stones, so forth. Says there's a tower back east somewhere. One that they built. Well, I don't see it here—" he turned back, "you remember the old man who always talked Swedish? Says Swedish ought to be our language, since the Swedes were here first."

"Swenson—?" I said. "You don't mean the old man with the two pretty girls?"

Bud raised his hand, the fingers spread, as if to put it over my face—then he drew it back, placed his index finger to his lips. I think he said sssshhhhh. We stood listening. At the top of the stairs the voices of the women, a little shrill above the radio, the sound of something frying, and behind me, in the darkness, a slow drip. I turned to look behind me, then I turned back.

"What's the trouble?" I said. "A new leak?" He had lowered his hand, nervously, to his hip. I didn't have the faintest notion what he had heard, or why he had started, until I noticed the color of his face. It was flushed. The color showed in his ears, and along his throat. Then, being a small town boy myself, I understood. I couldn't believe it—but that's another matter. I understood. Bud raised his hand to his face, then said— "Your voice. Maybe we shouldn't talk so loud." I waited, and he said— "You know—you know as well as I do, Clyde——"

"Are we talking about the same thing?" I said. He nodded hastily.

"You know as well as I do, Clyde," he said, "that there's no point in bringing up certain matters." He wiped his face and said, "No good—no good of any kind can come of it."

"God almighty, Bud—" I said, "all we did over there was play pinochle!"

When I said *pinochle* he raised one of Arbuthnot's books, as if to strike at something, then turned and walked with it behind the desk. He bent over as if looking for something on the floor. I could hear the radio again, above the voices of the women, and the fumbling noises Bud made in a tin box of nuts and bolts.

"I'm going to take a look around—Bud," I said, and came up to the kitchen, nodded at my wife, then opened the screen and walked out in the yard. A breeze had stirred up, showing the silver bottoms on the cottonwood leaves. Beyond the poplars, in the cool hollow, was the house of old man Swenson where twenty, thirty years ago he had raised eight or ten kids. In my time, two of them were husky blonde girls. What were they called? Esther was the big, soft, sweet one.

I walked around the house and out into the road where these thoughts, such as they were, would not corrupt Nellie, her home, or her man in the basement on his knees. From the road I could see the Swenson arbor, the vines now dead, like a tangle of barbed wire, and the concrete bird bath around which we had sat in the yard. Anything else? Not a thing. That was the hell of it.

It might be hard to explain that twenty years ago, a boy standing on this rise, or dreaming in this hollow, could close his eyes and hear music, music coming over water, as the saying goes. That the dream that might be lived, the girls that might be loved, were down there in the hollow, where the lights were blinking, just as they were there across the wide green lawns of West Egg. The Great Gatsby, don't forget, was born and raised out here. The great dream was clear in his mind long before he discovered Long Island Sound, that body of water just this side of Paradise. Gatsby is gone, but for twenty years now his unutterable dream, on its inflated rubber bier, will neither wash out to sea, sink, nor dissolve away. Like

Gatsby's resolves, in HOP-ALONG CASSIDY, it keeps turning up—

> No wasting time at shafters
> No more smokeing or chewing
> Read one improving book or magazine per week
> Save $5.00 (crossed out) $3.
> Be better to parents.

To this we could add

> Be true to the finest creature on God's Green earth.

I might have forgotten all of that if Bud Hibbard, my friend and an honest man, hadn't reminded me that the dream is written down. And that we both had been tempted, incurably. Nothing had happened—but the skin of that apple, the dream of that love had been so delicious that twenty years later Gatsby Hibbard knew he had sinned. He had gazed upon loveliness and desired her. In the tall glasses of root beer the ice had melted, but there was a breeze, and as you may remember it carried more than the odor of flowers on summer nights. Someone laughing in a hollow could be heard in the window on the rise. And this breeze was still blowing through the basement windows of Bud Hibbard's house.

Was this brown house in the hollow haunted with such ghosts? The blinds were drawn against the afternoon sun, and in the room upstairs, where a curtain was flapping, perhaps Mr. Swenson talked to his wife. Using the Swedish language, the speech of the discoverers. Belittling, once more, this fellow Columbus and his ilk.

Was it possible that Gatsby's Daisy had lived in such a house? That anything like music had been heard in the yard, a hundred miles from water, or that girlish laughter, if there was such a thing, had been blown anywhere? No man would believe it who had not come, as I just had, from the Hibbard basement, where sin and delight were preserved in amber, like the Lone Wolf. Where the sound of one word could bring back the music, the murmuring water music, the tinkling chimes on the porch, and the night as full of license as Cleopatra's barque.

Out here there was lust enough, there was mind and heart enough, but let there be no delight—no careening of the heart. Somewhere it had been resolved that the clapper be taken from the bell. That living, loving, and dying should be done soberly. As Orville Arbuthnot had warned —the careening of the globe held the key to our salvation, otherwise, like the mammoth, we were doomed for the long night of the ice. Like any major prophet, he had got around to speaking cryptically.

From a window at the front of the house my wife called, "We're ready to eat. Will you go and find your daughter?" As I nodded, she said, "The corn's on the table—I mean right now."

As I went along the fence the chickens passed the word along. Two roosters sat on the stoop to the hen house, like guards before a harem, and I could see the inmates, through the screen at the window, cock their heads at me. I cut across the back yard, giving a spin to the tire, then stopped to peer in the door of the garage.

"Oh honey—" I said.

Not a sound.

"The corn is on the table, Miss Muncy," I said.

"Did we come out here to be alone, or didn't we?"

she said. The voice came from behind, or from within, a large barrel of laying mash.

"You can be alone all evening," I said, "but right now your mother wants you for supper. It's customary, out here, to be together when we eat." I heard her sigh, then the canvas lid on the barrel stirred. After a moment it slipped back and I saw her golden hair, full of bran mash. "If your mother sees you like that," I said, "you may be alone for a long, long time."

"What was that place—" she said, "where you could be alone and left that way?"

"The outbilly?"

"Yes—" she said. "The outbilly. When I build a house we're going to have an outbilly."

"They've gone a bit out of fashion," I said.

"That wouldn't matter out here—would it?"

"Well, they're getting pretty up to date out here now, too," I said.

"Do you have to be modern—even when you have all this room?"

"Suppose you ask Nellie," I said, "you ask her what she thinks of that." She climbed out of the barrel, pulled her skirt below her knees. There was mash in the seat of her panties. She let it out.

As we walked toward the house she did what she could, in a ladylike way, to keep from scratching. "Were you and Mr. Hibbard once alike?" she said.

"We were boys together out here," I said.

"Think of that—" she said, "just think of that." Then— "City life has done quite a bit for you too, then." She put up her hand, took mine, and with a certain pomp led me into the kitchen. "Here we are," she said, "just a pair of city kids."

That was not so good, in some ways, as Nellie put down the butter she was melting and spread her white arms, like props, to lean on the sink. In the mirror beside the radio she looked at Bud, but he seemed busy, very busy, spoon feeding the baby from a can of strained prunes. He was still a little flushed and there were beads of moisture on his lip. "Ooops-a-daisy," he said, a little falsely, and emptied the spoon on the little one's face. It ran down the side of her nose into her open mouth.

"How's Miss Caddy these days?" I said, and dipped my ear of corn in the butter platter.

"Miss Catty?" said Nellie. I looked at Bud.

"Clint's wife—" said Bud. "Been so long since we called her Miss Caddy guess Nellie never heard it."

"You mean Mrs. Clinton Hibbard?"

"Yes, I guess that's who I mean," I said. I took a mouthful of corn, then said, "Well, anyhow, how is she?"

"She's poorly," said Nellie. "Nobody sees her anymore."

"Guess it's been a year or two," said Bud, "since she's been down from the second floor. Lives in her bedroom. Rest of the house is as good as closed up."

"That was quite a place in its time," I said.

"There's room in that house right now," said Nellie, "for two, three families the likes of us." She put her corn down, wiped her face, picked her corn up again. Her mouth was open when Bud looked at her. She closed it again.

"I suppose I'd better tell you," said Bud, "before somebody else does, that we don't get along. Guess we haven't for years."

"You didn't before we was married either," Nellie said.

"The Hibbards feudin'?" I said.

"No, the Hibbards ain't feudin'," said Bud.

"She's a Hibbard by law but not by anything else," Nellie said.

"I didn't really know her," I said. "She was always the lady at the front of the house. The only people I knew were Uncle Billie and Aunt Angie."

"Aunt Angie's deaf and blind," Nellie said, "but she tells everybody she'll live forever."

"Has already," said Bud. He stopped feeding the baby and looked at his wife. "Uncle Billie said that she'd live as long as that woman poor Clint married——"

"And then one week longer," Nellie said. That revived her appetite. She turned to the stove for another ear of corn.

"I take it Uncle Billie didn't manage that," I said.

"Don't think he cared," said Bud, "who died last—just so it wasn't Uncle Billie."

"Two, three years ago now—wasn't it, Bud?"

"In his sleep—" said Bud. "He came in from the garden—you know that garden at the side of the house?" I nodded. "Well, he came in from the garden, had his bowl of mush, then he went to lie down."

"When Aunt Angie shook him to pick her a melon he was dead."

"Turned out—" Bud said, "he hadn't wound his pocket watch that morning. Let it run down. Let himself run down the same way. Doc said it was so close God himself wouldn't know who ran down first."

We ate corn. This was a thing to think about. Uncle Billie was tangled up in my mind with old Farmer Brown and Bre'r Rabbit, an old man who chased rabbits and boys like myself out of his garden patch. One time, in the dark, I threw a clod at a him. When I knew him he was living in overalls with a frazzled patch at the front, where he leaned on the hoe, the rake, and the handle of the lawn mower. There was a rumor, when I was a boy, that Uncle Billie came to town with a coach and four, with a lady wearing satin, and one wearing velvet, on each arm. The one in yellow satin was Aunt Angie, and the one wearing velvet pined away in the Undertaker's House you could see from the road near Grand Island. Her lamp could be seen when you drove by at night. I don't know where I got that story, as Uncle Billie was quite an old skinflint, giving us boys three cents a pound for good tinfoil. Everybody knew he made his snuff money out of us.

"Only trouble we have with Aunt Angie—" said Bud, "is we can't get her out of her shoes. Need heels and soles, but can't get her out of them. She's scared to death we'll take those shoes and she'll never see 'em again."

"It doesn't matter what it is," Nellie said, "she likes it better the way it once was. It doesn't matter if it's shoes, babies, buttons, or what it is."

"Them heels is just as round, like your thumb—" said Bud, and put his thumb up in the air. "If she did anymore than slide around that kitchen we'd be scared to death." He wiped his face with the towel and said— "Were you here when they put in the toilet?"

I shook my head. At the back of the yard, splattered

with shadows, I could see Aunt Angie's outbilly. She kept it locked. She didn't want, she said, any writin' on the seats.

"Well, you know what Miss Caddy thought of that privy—" I nodded my head. "But when she tore it down Aunt Angie refused to use the one in the house. She said she'd use Uncle Billie's garden before she'd use that. So Clint had to put one under the kitchen—there's a fruit cellar there, you know. Guess she goes up and down those stairs two, three times a day."

"Tub down there too—" said Nellie, "but no way to get water in or out of it. Rubber stopper in it. But you have to pan the water in and out."

"Guess she does it," said Bud. "Anyhow she takes all her baths down there.

"I take it they're still feudin'?" I said.

"Maybe nobody should say this—" said Nellie, and looked across at Bud, licking her mouth.

"Anybody can see it," said Bud, "the old lady's going to win out."

"You can't go—" Nellie said, "from the front of the house to the kitchen. She keeps the door locked. If you want to see her you have to go out in back."

"How did Uncle Billie take this?" I said.

"Don't think he really noticed," said Bud. "He had his mush, his garden, and his seed catalogues. In the last twenty years don't think I ever saw him at the front of the house."

I didn't think it was worth explaining to my wife that this Clinton Hibbard was Bud's uncle, and that Aunt Angie and Uncle Billie were his grandparents. They seemed to have those names before we came along, and

[83]

we stuck to them. Bud was not a favorite of theirs, not being their notion of a real Hibbard, and I think Aunt Angie figured that her boy Clinton was the last of the line. When he had no children, she decided that ended it.

"Some people say that what was too much for Uncle Billie, is keepin' Aunt Angie alive—" Nellie looked from Bud, who kept his eyes on his plate, to my wife.

"Miss Caddy?" I said.

"If that's what you want to call her," Nellie said.

Looking at my wife I said, "Miss Caddy, Clint's wife, was from southern Indiana."

"She was from the south, the deep south. She admitted it herself."

"Before she closed the house," Bud said, "used to see her in there paintin' on china. Place was a mess, but she seemed to find time for that."

"With her own hands," Nellie said, "she crocheted little jackets you put on water glasses. They sit around by themselves. She dipped them in sugar syrup to make them stiff."

"Uncle Billie said she put on rubber gloves to cut a flower——"

"Or use her sprinklin' can. You could see her in the flowers with the black rubber gloves and the red sprinklin' can. One of her hats without a crown, to show her golden hair, and the brim as wide as a parasol."

That was quite a picture. We stopped eating to look at it. The flowers on the sunny side of the house and this strange woman, this foreigner, with the black rubber gloves, the tuft of golden hair, and the red sprinkling can. Perhaps a pair of shears on a loop of yellow ribbon, not in her hand, no, that right hand glided at her side, idly, like the fin of a tropical fish. Neither extended nor withdrawn, but suggesting that a friendly arm, or a padded chair back, might be useful, even necessary, to lean upon. So that there was always something, or somebody, at her side. Somebody leaving or approaching, and at these times the hand was in suspension, fluttering, like a disturbed butterfly. Then settling—or rather pausing, tentatively. These were things I knew, as the hand had rested on my head. In such a manner that I couldn't tell you the feel of the rubber glove, or what the face beneath the parasol hat was like. I never saw it. I doubt if I managed to look toward it. For something like this, for a woman who could stand in a gown of light, with a red sprinkling can, Clinton Hibbard, I knew in my heart, had married her. Men and boys not so easily dazzled spoke of her face as long, like a goat, with great wet eyes and a nose with very large pores. That might be. I never looked at her. Now and then, as she moved away on her high heels, her weak ankles rocking, I saw that her feet were large and seemed to trouble her. The brick walk, the gravel path, the wooden slats or whatever it was, was not, plainly, what she was accustomed to walking on. It gave her trouble. She seemed ready to falter at every step. One hand she pressed to her throat, the other swam at her side, the fingers extended, as a sleepwalker will enter an unfamiliar room.

"You say she isn't well?" my wife said.

"According to Doc," Bud said, "guess she's on her last legs. Can't get her to move around. Guess if you won't move around there's nothing he can do."

"For awhile there was a girl named Chloe looked after her, cooked her meals. Then she was gone. I suppose she went back where they both came from."

Twenty years ago, when I was back to see the Swenson girls, and walk around the streets, I saw Miss Caddy, in a feathered hat and boa, on her front porch. That was about the time that Aunt Angie moved from the front of the house into the kitchen, taking with her the two dresses, the one hat and pair of shoes that she had come with. When Clinton Hibbard died—a cigar in his mouth, the Kansas City papers spread over his face—Aunt Angie closed and locked the door to the kitchen, and that was that. Miss Caddy went on living in the other twelve rooms, painting china, wearing rubber gloves, but more and more inclined to do her living in bed. The couch drawn to the front window, where, if she wanted to, she could look out. And where—if the lights were on—others could see in.

"You think Aunt Angie would remember me?" I said.

"Don't she speak of Clyde now and then, Bud?"

"She'll talk your leg off about anything you mention. If she ever forgot anything nobody's ever learned what it was."

"She can't see you any too well," said Nellie. "She just smells you out. Don't think she even looks."

"We thought of putting up a fence," Bud said, "to keep her from falling into that new cellar. But Doc said any new-fangled thing like that would just tangle her up. Just finding it there would throw her off schedule, get her upset."

Tapping on the table, Nellie said, "She hasn't fallen once yet."

"She's like a snout in the trough," said Bud, "if you just leave her alone. People doing something for her is the only thing to worry about."

"If I thought she'd remember me—" I said.

"She'll tell you all about yourself," said Nellie.

"But not tonight—" said my wife. She looked at me directly and said, "Didn't you say we had to reach the river tonight?"

"Mrs. Muncy—" Nellie said, "you'll do no such thing."

"We've really got to get on," Peg said.

"There's not a thing you could do," Nellie said, "but begin to look for one of those bed-buggy tourist cabins. Along the tracks. Every last one of them is along the tracks."

"Mrs. Muncy—" said Bud, looking right at her. "I ain't seen Clyde here for fifteen years. We got plenty room. We got a whole house right here, huh Nellie?"

"Why sure," said Nellie.

"I don't mind the trains—" I said, for my wife's benefit, "but these new juke boxes get under my skin."

"Night and day—" said Nellie, "but you only hear it at night."

"We got all the room in the world right here," said Bud. "The kids can sleep in the garage. When it gets too hot they sleep out there anyway."

I thought that would settle it, but never underestimate your wife.

"You men have so much to talk about," said Peg, "why don't the two of you lie out there and do it? You could talk all night. It wouldn't bother anyone."

"Why, that's an idea, Clyde—" said Bud. "How about it?"

"I'm really a little pooped," I said. "I didn't sleep any too well last night."

"For a good night's sleep," said Bud, "give me a nice cool night in the garage."

"That sounds wonderful," said Peg. "Just what Clyde loves."

I got up from the table and said, "Well, I guess I better run along if I'm going to see Aunt Angie."

"You know how to get there?" said Bud. I nodded my head. "That was going to be some neighborhood," said Bud, "but it didn't pan out. Nothing happened. There's a dump there now, right under the light at the end of the road."

"The town went the other way," Nellie said.

"The paving went east," said Bud, "so I guess they thought that was where the town was going."

"But it didn't," said Nellie.

"No, it didn't go anywhere. Just a bunch of lights out there in the dark."

"When you think of a woman like her—" said Nellie, "a southern woman. I suppose she finds it lonely."

"She used to walk along—" said Bud, "carryin' a parasol."

"To see Aunt Angie," I said, "what do I do, go around in back?"

"The front's locked," said Bud. "You go by in the daytime and you'd think the place was shut up. Night time you can see Caddy's light in the room upstairs. That's where she stays. Doc has a key of his own, lets himself in and out."

"Mr. Purdy—" Nellie said, "says she plays a lot of phonograph records."

"The one with the big horn?" I said.

"That's the one," said Bud. I opened the screen and Bud went on— "Go around in back, around the rain barrel, and you'll see the lamp in the old man's room. Oil lamp. She won't have anything to do with anything new. If Mr. Purdy isn't there, tap on the glass in the old man's bird box. It's right there in the window. It's where she gets her mail——"

"And her milk," Nellie said.

"With the old man gone she has troubles with the squirrels. They get into the bird box and eat the seeds. They even get into the house. Chewed a hole in the window on the other side."

"She just sits there," Nellie said, "day in and day out, her cane in her lap, waitin' for one of those danged squirrels to put in his head. When he does, she biffs him with the cane."

"Providin' she isn't asleep," said Bud.

I closed the screen, and crossing the yard I heard the boy reminding his mother that his father didn't like to go places alone. *This* time he would just have to, his mother said.

I parked my car under the elms between the alley and the culvert, where, as a boy, I stowed away most of my Chautauqua handbills. A piece of tattered asphalt went down to the corner, where the street light hung, the white globe soiled, like a table cloth, with the lapping rings where mudballs had struck, then dropped. Beyond the light a battered sign read DUMP, and several rusty cans, from the pile behind, had been thrown or kicked out in the road. A wisp of yellow smoke rose from a tire burning in the pit. Near the edge of the pit a small boy, a rifle over his arm, lowered the gun to watch me cross the street. A small basket of rats, swarming with flies, sat at his side. I raised my hand, in the manner of my father, wagging it like a semaphore at the wrist, but the boy turned to see who I was waving at. Nobody. My hand was down when he looked back.

Miss Caddy's place, as we used to call it, occupied most of a city block, once Uncle Billie got around to putting his garden in. A wooden house, with windows that rose from the floor to nearly the ceiling, the shutters were all on the inside, rather than the out. This was just one thing but it made it clear, and spared you the trouble of looking for others, that the house, like Caddy, had been imported—it was not grown here. This was such an accepted thing that its real strangeness had gone unnoticed, like the strangeness, I suppose, of Miss Caddy herself. One remarked her rubber gloves, and let it go at that. I had lived in this yard as a boy without remarking the wooden fence, like a bit of lacework, that went across the front of the house. If it had been around the yard I would have seen it, time and again I would have had to climb it, but the yard was wide open, this fence was just part of the house. With her sprinkling can Miss Caddy could stand in front of her house, but still within it, and look across the wide, park-like yard at the town and the street. In that yard, all summer, were the heavy wire wickets, marked with little flags of white ribbon, and the heavy banded posts of her imported set of croquet. The club heads metal-ringed, to keep them from splitting, and both the balls and the clubs lined up in a rack, like artillery equipment, at the edge of the porch. Because of the strength of these wickets, which would trip Uncle Billie when he chased us, we cruised through the garden, or around the shady side of the house. In spite of the ribbons, they were hard to see in the dark. Other times the front lawn was used for birthdays—other people, it seemed, always had them—and Japanese lanterns were strung between the elm trees and the house. On a quilting frame, propped up in the yard, young people from Lincoln, and even Omaha, were blind-folded and told to pin on the donkey's tail. Older people —in their teens, that is—sat in the swings, or the creaking hammocks, or blocked the stairs where they gathered to eat ice cream.

Most of these evenings, however, Bud and I spent around in back, with Aunt Angie and Uncle Billie, turning the crank on two or three ice cream freezers. This work paid well, as Aunt Angie never troubled to scrape along the bottom, or count the slices of cake put out on the trays. Later we would help Uncle Billie with the lanterns, which collapsed like accordions, and were put in a chest with the donkey and the masks some of the young men wore. Several times a year somebody was married, and Mr. Hibbard himself, wearing a protector, would shoot Roman candles at paper birds hung in the trees. The birds would have ladies' names, and it was said that *that* lady was sure to be next. These evenings were long, and every summer there were many, but delicate as she seemed to be Miss Caddy was the first one, and then the last one, out on the porch. Always with her hand out, gently, like a person on thin ice. Or she would play the piano—little snatches, she called them—wearing black gloves without fingers, and playing, it was said, only on the black keys. And she would leave the lights on, all over the house, until Clinton

Hibbard, the District Attorney, had come down from Lincoln to see that her party had gone all right. He drove a Franklin, with an air-cooled motor—which I was led to think was why he left the motor running, as he seldom stayed. He was never in the house very long. But while he was there we sat in the Franklin, on the front seat. On both sides of the seat were horns of polished brass, in the shape of a bugle, with a red rubber bulb too large for my hand. To squeeze this bulb I had to use both of them. This report—made when he drove us home—signaled that one more great event was over, and that Clinton Hibbard, Bud, and myself were on our way home.

There was a light, as Bud had predicted, in the front room upstairs. I tried to recall the face of Miss Caddy, but the brim of a hat, or the shadow of a feather, seemed to come between me and her voice, which I remembered as clear. It was reported that she had once cried—"Doggie, doggie, doggie!" in a bell-like voice, at what she had seen, in a troop of trained dogs, at the Chautauqua. Somehow, I found that easy to believe. The woman I thought I knew, the girl Clinton Hibbard believed he had married, would have cried *Doggie, doggie, doggie,* in just such a fashion, and nothing else. Rising from her seat on the aisle, perhaps rocking a bit, in the loose sawdust, her hand half raised, like a woman at the stern of a boat. Crying this thing, distracting dogs and patrons, then sitting down. Anyhow, it explained why this fellow Clinton had married her. I had never wondered—as everybody else seemed to—what he had seen in this childless woman, or why he couldn't see it without marrying her. Clinton Hibbard, a man who had once ridden, so it was said, on a Sioux squaw's horse, had turned his back on one frontier to face another one. Both were passing. He wanted to preserve one of them. He decided on Miss Caddy, the cloak of light with the red sprinkling can.

A loud racket, like a shutter clattering, made me jump. I was wading through the garden, weedy now, but stopped and turned toward the racket, the large bird-box fastened to the window of the old man's room. A large, moth-eaten squirrel sat on top of it. He was biding his time, his mouth full, while a pointed stick, the sharp end of a cane, rattled up and down, back and forth, inside the bird box. Then the cane withdrew, and I heard the lid snap down. There was no light in the room, but as I reached the window, where Bud said I should rap, I saw a match flare inside somewhere. After a moment I saw the wick, the flame crawling over the carbon tip, then the sudden glow as the chimney was lowered, the flame shot up. The fluted top of the chimney was cracked and I could see the crisp hairs, like watch springs, that had been stretched taut across the top to test the height of the flame. The bowl of the lamp was clear, the yellowed color of isinglass, and the wick floated like a bottled specimen in the kerosene. Aunt Angie stood with her back to me. She stood with her legs spread, humped over, her arms akimbo like a dancing bear, with just the white knob of her hair above her shoulder blades. In her left hand she held the cane, which she tapped on the floor like a blindman, wheeling slowly, like an engine on a roundhouse platform. As she turned with the lamp I could see that the room, this room, was not part of the house—that she had moved it back, settled it, in her own time. This room might have been off the kitchen on the farm. A rocker, a straight-backed chair, a table covered with a red and white cloth, and the cloth covered with all the things she might reach for. A sewing kit made from a box of Uncle Billie's cigars, a pair of shears, a glasses case, and old copies of the *Junction Call*. In the cupboard several cups without handles, heavy ivory plates with cracks like a beard, and a glass sugar bowl—the good one—full of buttons and small change. The woman coming toward me belonged in this room. She was wearing black, and the once-white lace at the cuffs, and around the collar, was the saddle-leather color of her face. An apron hung from her throat like a banner, the strings flapping. Her mouth was greasy, and midway she raised her head, as if she had seen me, and I saw that her lips were moving—she was talking to herself. She had done that years before—in the midst of our talk we would see her conversing, carrying on a discussion with worthy people who were not there. Her head wagging, suddenly turning to peer out the window—or to close our discussion with some cryptic remark. I didn't rap—I let her sit down, a business that took some nice calculation, and an abiding trust that things were where she had left them, and unchanged. The drop into the chair set her to rocking, which she seemed to like, her head went back, and above the creak of a loose board I could hear her voice. *Abide With Me*. She was singing it with her eyes softly closed.

I let her finish one verse, then I tapped on the glass. She cocked her head, waited, and I rapped again. Opening the lid to the bird-box she said, "That you Mr. Purdy?"

"No, Aunt Angie—" I said, then stopped. Who was I?

I was the little Muncy boy. "You remember the little Muncy boy?" I said.

"Will's boy?" she said. I had forgotten that I was.

"Yes, Aunt Angie—" I said, "Will's boy."

"Well, I declare—" she said, and set herself to rocking again. She rocked a half dozen times, then said, "I suppose by now you're grown—can you read?"

"Yes—" I said.

"Was expectin' Mr. Purdy. You want to come in and read to me?"

"How do I get in?" I said.

"You and Clinton," she said. "You forget which side your face is on."

"It's been a long time, Aunt Angie," I said.

"You think it's been any shorter for me?" She leaned back, dropping her hands to the arms of the chair. After a moment she leaned forward, her right hand fumbling in a Buster Brown Shoe Box that contained postcards and sunflower seeds for the cardinals. She put two of the seeds in her mouth, nibbled on them. Then I realized she had forgotten me.

"Oh, Aunt Angie—" I said, and tapped again.

"That you Mr. Purdy?"

"This is Will's boy, Clyde—" I said. "Should I go around to the back door and come in?"

"What a thing to be askin' your Aunt Angie," she said.

I walked around to the back porch door, tried the latch, found it open. Inside I had to squeeze around the ice box, which had a strong smell.

"Mr. Purdy brings himself up a chair," she said. Then —"You wouldn't know where Mr. Purdy is?"

"No, Aunt Angie—" I said, and took a straight-backed chair from the wall. The veneer on the seat was peeling, and I suddenly remembered that one of these chairs used to pinch my seat as a boy. As I walked toward her she moved the light so that it fell on my face.

"Don't see a thing," she said, "guess I'm blind as a bat."

"You're looking pretty good, Aunt Angie," I said.

"You men!" she said, and wet her lips. I could not see her eyes, behind her steel-rimmed glasses, the lenses the color of flecked isinglass, but I remembered the mole, like a large potato eye, on her forehead. Moving the lamp back she said, "You say you can read?"

"Let me try it," I said, and reached for the copy of the *Junction Call* in the spokes of her rocker.

"I don't get around anymore," she said, "so I have to read."

"Like anything in particular?" I said, and opened the paper to the word Auctions.

"What you mean by that?"

"Anything—" I said, "you're especially interested in."

"What business is that of yours?" she said.

"All I'm trying to find out," I said, "is which one of these items you'd like me to read."

"I never thought I'd live to see the day," she said, "your Aunt Angie would find herself talked to like that." She wagged her head, then said, "Where you learn things like that?"

"I'm a city-boy—" I said, "I guess we learn them in the city."

"I could've told you—" she said. "Omaha-Omaha— that's all I hear."

[96]

"I'm not living in Omaha, Aunt Angie—" I said.

"Where then?"

"We're living in New York." She leaned forward, bracing herself, to look at my face.

"Clinton was there. Never done him a bit of good."

I turned back to the paper, an article entitled LEE FLYNN DEAD, but there was a knock on the door before I could start.

"There's Purdy," she said. "Ask him in."

"Come in," I called, and watched an elderly man squeeze around the ice box, step into the light. When he saw me he took off a light straw hat. In his left hand he held a green glass bowl with a saucer over the top.

"Well—" he said, "callers?"

"Mr Purdy—" the old lady said, "this is Will's boy."

"So—?" said Mr. Purdy. He came forward into the light. He put his hat on the chair, the glass bowl on the table, and then, absently, loosened the button on his pants. Prepared to sit down. But he remained standing. "So—" he repeated.

"I was a boy out here," I said, and cleared my throat to go on, as it was quite a topic.

"Libby made some custard," Mr. Purdy said, and turned from me to the table. He took the saucer from the bowl, crossed the room to take a spoon from a glass in the cupboard, then came back to place the bowl in her lap. When she put up her hand for the spoon he gave it to her.

"I've always said," the old lady said, "there's nothin' like Libby Purdy's custard." Then she seemed to forget us. With the handle of the spoon she cleaned the trough in her teeth. Mr. Purdy stood with his hands on his hips, then he noticed he was standing, drew up a chair. He had slipped his barefeet into a pair of old shoes, tucked the laces in the top. The soles were green and wet from his walk across the grass.

"You just passin' through?" he said, and tipped his chair back, hooked his thumb in his belt.

"I suppose that's what you'd call it," I said, but I didn't go on. He didn't seem to be listening. He put a match in his mouth, and at the same time made a rasping sound in his short white beard. A white moustache was cropped close to his upper lip.

"Seem any different," he said, "seem about the same?"

"Well, yes and no—" I said.

"She hasn't changed much," he said, and nodded his head toward her, as if she were sleeping. She spooned up the custard with the bowl right below her mouth. After each spoonful her plates clattered like the cane in the bird-box. Perhaps she heard this noise, as she stopped, twice, as if to listen for it. "This young fellow read to you yet?" he said.

"No, he didn't," she said. "Don't think he can." She lowered her head, her eyes lidded, to make it clear it was a joke. Mr. Purdy took the paper from my lap and sat himself so the light was behind him.

"You hear about Lee?" he said.

"Nobody has read me a thing," she said.

Clearing his throat, putting the match back in his vest, Mr. Purdy read the following—

LEE FLYNN DEAD

Resident of fifty-four years
mourned by wife, Adelaide and
five daughters—

[98]

He paused, moving back the glasses that were low on his nose. Aunt Angie had turned from him, from both of us, and tipped forward with her head into the bird-box, as if she had heard, or had seen something there. But she was looking through it, as her eyes seemed to follow something in the street. As I leaned forward she said— "There it goes—there it goes!" but in the dark street I could see nothing passing. No one stood under the light, no cloud of dust rose from the road. In the heavy summer air over the corner bugs flew in and out, like a tangled ball of yarn, and the locusts sounded like a siren running down.

"Yes, there it goes—" said Mr. Purdy, and winked at me.

Aunt Angie rocked forward, following with her eyes something that made the turn at the corner, at a slow pace, and then moseyed out of town. "There it goes—there it goes—" she repeated, and then— "the Dead Wagon." She took one more good look at it, then rocked back, as if away from us. Her arms relaxed, her head tipped forward, and before the rocker had stopped its movement, or the creak had left the floor, Aunt Angie was asleep. The suds of lace, at her chin, began to blur a little as she snored.

"Well, that's that—" said Mr. Purdy, and reached across her lap for the lamp, turned down the wick. He took the custard bowl from her lap, found the spoon in her apron pocket, and set the lamp in the cast-iron bracket on the wall.

"Is she O-kay?" I said.

"She'll nap—" he said, "for a little while, then she'll wake up an' go to bed. Does this every night. She's quite an old timer now, you know."

"I know that—" I said, and followed him outside. He put the spoon in his pocket to keep it from rattling. As we crossed the yard I said, "What's all this about the Dead Wagon?"

"That's a hearse," he said. "Used to call it the Dead Wagon, you know."

"No, I didn't know—" I said.

"Well, they did—" he said. I waited for him to go on. "Is that all?" I said.

"You mean her seein' it out the window?" he said. I nodded. "Oh well—" he said, "she's been seein' that wagon for thirty years." He looked at me. "Must have seen it first when you was a kid."

"I guess I missed that," I said.

"Nothing serious—" he said. "you know old people." I felt he was smiling but I couldn't see his face. "Your Uncle Billie told me—" he stopped to put the match back in his mouth, "that when she was just a kid they took her mother away in a wagon like that. Then her father. Guess it made quite an impression on her."

"But you know—" I said, "I got the feeling that she liked it——"

Mr. Purdy had already turned away. I watched him wade through the ditch, walk slowly into the light. Under the light he turned and said— "You know that one about peein' in the road?"

"I guess not," I said.

> "Strawberry shortcake,
> Huckleberry pie,
> Pee in the road
> An' you'll get a sty."

"You don't know that?" he said, then— "I just wondered what you thought of it. Never had a sty myself—" he said, and walked into the dark.

Aunt Angie's Dead Wagon had made the turn to the right, and I made this turn, driving along the tracks, wondering if the old man was deliberately pulling my leg. This is a hard thing to determine out here. I was five or six miles west of town—I could see the lights of Lone Tree down the tracks—before I remembered that my family was back in Junction. I turned the car around, started back. At the edge of town the Neon sign of the WEE BLUE INN clicked on and off, and the old Buick touring, with the sack in the seat, was still parked in the yard. I thought a beer might cool me off a little and pulled in alongside the Buick, letting the motor idle while I listened to the juke-box tune. In the front seat of the old man's car, his head propped on the sack of mash, was an old dog with large, sad, bloodshot eyes. When he caught my eye his heavy tail thumped the seat. One corner of his lip was sucked in, held there by a long, yellow tooth, as if in his sorrow he had forgotten about it. My troubles, whatever they had been, seemed pretty small.

I'd say the reason I like cats better than dogs is that they go about their own catty business, while any dog at all is a better man than I am half the time. This was one of those times and I got in the bar, walked across the dark room toward the chrome legs of a stool, seated myself on it, before I noticed the old man at my side. One stool away, a bottle of Budweiser, half poured, in his hand. His dark face looked green in the cold light from the bar. Level on his head was a hat with a bill, a heavy cord around the crown, and a nautical emblem askew at the front. He was facing the juke box, a plumbing system of bubbling soda water, but something in his expression reminded me of Aunt Angie. He was seeing things—he wiped the suds from his moustache, focused on them.

"Think St. Joe was ahead—" he continued, to no one in particular, "think they was ahead two of these markers to one." Then turning to me he said, "Game was played in nine of these innings—first you come to bat and then you went out. St. Joe had two of these markers and Lincoln had one." He stopped there to recall the scene, twang his nose.

"I get it, Pop—" the barman said, "two to one."

"These St. Joe men was just as quick as a rabbit, hoppin' around, runnin' the bases, wherever the Lincoln man hit it was where the St. Joe man was. Come the ninth inning St. Joe was ahead, two markers to one. First thing you know the Lincoln man hit it right down the middle, not a man there to touch it. St. Joe men hopped, but they couldn't get a hand on it. Next man hit it right down the line and around the far corner—" he turned to point out the window, "around the far corner came another marker, like a Jack rabbit. Never seen a man so scared in his life. Next man like to hit it clean out of the park. Click, he went, like a branch crackin'—that was all for St. Joe."

The old man tipped up the bottle, peered into it.

"How long back you see this game?" the barman said.

"Was in St. Joe for the hog sale," he said. "Think it was twenty one." He poured the rest of the beer in his glass, tipped the glass over his head.

"What'll you have, Bub?" said the barman, and turned

to me. In the quiet I could hear the record in the juke box drop.

"Nineteen hundred and twenty one," said the old man. "Things was lookin' up."

I leaned on the cigar case and said, "Maybe I'll take two of these White Owls." He reached the box from beneath the case, I took two cigars. "What are they worth now?" I said.

"Nine straight now, Bub—" he said.

"In nineteen twenty one," I said, "they were two for fifteen." Off hand I would say that barman, from the way he looked at me, was still pinned in a diaper in nineteen twenty one. I took my change and came out in the cinder yard, facing the dog, before I remembered I had gone in there for a drink.

"How ya boy," I said, and scratched a match on the Buick, lit the White Owl.

On my way back I drove through the town, past Miss Caddy's house where her light was still burning, but Aunt Angie's window, and Uncle Billie's bird-box, were dark. There were no lights in Mr. Purdy's house across the street. The draft off the dump blew along the tracks like the smoke from the ditch grass, a sour smell in the air, and perhaps a new odor in the rooms of the Western Hotel. I drove past the Hotel to see if the blinds were drawn. They were. Through the lobby window I could see two oak rockers, a potted palm, and a night light burning at the back, over the desk. A man's socked feet were propped on the desk, and on the wall behind, under the clock, a calendar view of the Overland Limited in the Royal Gorge.

When I drove up to the house the drive was empty, Bud had parked his car in the yard, and a curtain of cheese-cloth hung across the door to the garage. I switched off the lights and got out of the car. Except for the night light over the sink the house was dark, quiet, and I could hear the whine of the refrigerator belt. I took my pajamas out of my bag, then sat down on the bumper to scratch one or two mosquito bites. On second thought I decided to wear my pajama pants, but to leave on my shirt, as the sleeves were long. Carrying my shoes I raised the cheese-cloth, stepped into the garage. There was a cot stretched before me and I put out my hand, in a friendly fashion, to what I thought was Bud's head. It struck me that he seemed to have quite a bit of hair.

"This is me," said Nellie.

"For Pete's sake, Nellie—" I said, "pardon me."

"You're sleepin' inside," Nellie said, "we decided to switch around." She turned on her side to scratch a bite, rolled back again. "You and the Missus are sleepin' in-side," she said.

"Now look here, Nellie—" I said.

"SSsssshhhh—" she said. "Bud's sleepin'."

I stood there and she turned back to the bite.

"Well—" I said.

"Watch you don't step on the kids, they're sleepin' on the floor."

"Sure—" I said. "Well, good night—Nellie."

"Good night, Clyde," she said.

Carrying my shoes I walked across the yard to the house. I stepped on a marble, which was right there be-tween my toes when I looked for it—one of these knobby

numbers we used to call crockies. I found the kids—two
of mine and one of Bud's—asleep on Nellie's blue broadloom rug, heat rising from the evening's bites, the morning's sunburn. I undressed in the bathroom, tossing my
clothes over the new shower curtain rack, then went into
the bedroom where I had slept as a kid. Bud and I, lying
on top of the covers as it always seemed to be summer,
facing the window that looked straight down the tracks.
Down the spur was the switch with the red and green
light, the dark frame of the cattle loader, and the house
of the man who was known to have married a city girl.
A little thing, as Aunt Angie had said, soft as the fur for
kitten's britches, married to a great ham-handed lump of
a man. After a day and a night in this man's house she
was gone. Nobody blamed her. Everybody knew she was
a pretty thing, with soft white hands, accustomed to having the food she ate brought to her. Accustomed to having
her water poured—as I had seen it poured through the
diner windows—unaccustomed to the summer whiff of the
cattle loader. No, nobody blamed her, everybody knew
that the eastbound freight, at seven-twenty some morning,
would have a passenger on the platform of the caboose.
From there she could look right down the tracks at the
house itself, the lamp in the window, and the lump of a
man shadowed on the cracked blind. It was known that
he ate corn bread and milk from a water glass.

"Did you have a lovely time?" my wife said. When
you're as old as I am you learn to handle remarks like
that. You go to the window, raise the blind, then lower
it an inch. You stand there more or less lost in thought.
"Well—" she repeated, making it clear that there was a

good deal on her mind. That was too bad. I had hoped she would listen to me.

"You tell me your dreams," I said, "then I will tell you mine."

"If I ever again—" she said, foreseeing that time very clearly, "get into something like this it will be for the last time." That was rather weakly put, but I didn't mention it. But I could see that I hadn't come back too soon.

"Just be glad," I said, "that you're not lying out there in mosquito Junction. I could hear them scratching." She said nothing. "Well—" I said.

"You and your loving son," she said.

"Hmmmmm——"

"I suppose you know she baked a pie?"

"Huh-uh," I said.

"Well, she did. A chocolate pie just because *he* asked for it."

"Hmmmm——"

"When the time comes for the pie she cuts him a piece, nearly a quarter of it, and Mr. Hibbard says, 'Well boy, how does that taste?'"

"Yes—?" I said.

"'Like soap—' he said, and spit it out in his plate."

I raised the blind another inch or so, looked down the tracks.

"What did it taste like?" I said.

"Like soap," she said. "He said it tasted like soap. It tasted like soap. What am I supposed to do?"

"I suppose you could eat it," I said.

"Why do you think I'm just lying here?" she said.

I came back and sat down on the bed, took off my socks.

"I don't like New York, I don't want to live there, I don't want my children to have to grow up there, but when she asked me how in the world I could stand it—well, I told her."

"Yes——"

"I told her I lived in New York because Junction was like this." A train went by, the coach lights a band of light on the wide plain, and after a moment the curtains stirred, the blind flapped on the sill. "I told her I'd live and die in New York before I'd ask my husband, or my kids, to try and live and breathe in a god-forsaken hole like this. I didn't want to hurt her but I couldn't help it. It just came out."

"Well, I guess you told her," I said.

"Do you think it's true?"

"I don't know anymore," I said. "I do and I don't."

"Did *you* tell somebody something?"

I tried to think. I hadn't done so well. I had the feeling that the old men had told me. "I saw the old lady," I said. "She's the spit and image of Grandmother Cropper."

"You didn't see this Miss Caddy?"

"No—" I said.

"I've been lying here thinking what a simply godawful life that must have been. Alone in that house. All these bitter people hating her."

"I don't know about that," I said. "You can't be too sure about that."

"Well, I'm sure of it—" she said, and I think she was. But I was not at all sure of it myself. I got up once to turn off the faucet tapping on a saucer, left in the sink, and look through the narrow window over the sink at the town. It was early morning, the street lights hung like so many scattered planets, lamps without shadows, and with just enough light to remain in themselves, quiet and framed. There was a time in the evening that was the same. But the morning was clear, and the roads that led out in the morning led back when the evening lights came on. Led back along the tracks, where the grass was smoking, back along the dump where the garbage was burning, back to where you stood erect upon your own shadow, shadowless in the street.

BOOK TWO

THE ATTIC

THE ATTIC

The dull buzz of the telephone woke me up. I lay
there until I remembered that Bud and Nellie were out
in the garage, and until I was sure that my wife would
let it ring. Then I got up and headed for the kitchen,
stepping over the kids. As I lifted the receiver I noticed
the clock, and that it was just 6:20 AM, before I heard
a familiar voice over the phone.

"This you Muncy?"

"Yes—" I said, "this is Clyde Muncy."

"This is Purdy. Sorry to get you up but I think we
may have some trouble over here."

"Trouble?" I said.

"Is Bud there, Muncy?"

"He's asleep," I said, "—right at this point."

"Well, you'll do—thing is," he stopped to cough into
the receiver, "thing is, I just noticed her light was still
on."

"Aunt Angie?" I said.

"No, Caddy—" he said.

"She forget to turn it off?" I said. I was wondering
what there was about his calling her Caddy.

"No, Caddy don't forget—" He seemed to be speaking
of an old pet, lovable and hopeless. "That's just the point,
I've never known Caddy to forget her light."

"Oh—" I said.

"Last time she did we nearly lost her."

"Heart?" I said.

"They call it heart," he said.

"You hold on a moment," I said, "I'll step in and wake Bud."

"I better get over there," he said, "just thought I'd better call and tell you it's burnin'. He'll know. He'll remember what that was like."

"O-kay—" I said, "I'll tell him."

"First thing I did was call the Doc. He's got a key, you know. Now I'm waitin' for him. He ought to be here any minute now."

"Well, you keep us posted," I said.

"Call you back as soon as I know," he said, and hung up. I stood there with the phone until it buzzed, put it back on the hook. There was no sign of life in the garage, the cheesecloth curtain billowed in the draft and a cat with a splattered black and brown face sat at the head of the drive.

"Oh Clyde—" said my wife. I wet my face at the sink, walked back to the door. "Something's happened," she said. "I know it. Who is it?"

"That saves me a lot of explanation—" I said.

"The old lady—" said my wife. "I just knew it."

"Wrong—" I said, "as usual."

"Then the young one."

"That's a pretty safe system," I said, "if you live in a small enough town."

"If you don't tell me right now," she said, "and without any foolishness, I won't listen." She rolled over to face the wall. Then she rolled back. "I'm listening—" she said.

"There may be some trouble with Caddy—" I said, "her light is still on."

"Do people call her Caddy?"

"They do now."

"Why didn't he go see?"

"First you get the Doctor," I said. "The Doctor has a key. Then you go look."

"All alone like that," said Peg. "That's criminal."

"She's been alone for nearly thirty years," I said.

"You think that makes it any better?" I went into the bathroom, put on my pants and shirt. "They're cruel," she said, "just cruel, they can't stand people with more lives than their own."

"Just remember," I said, "that all we have is a night-light burning. That's all. Suppose we wait and see what it's lighting up."

"Why can't they leave her alone!"

"I'm not bothering her," I said.

"You are," she said, "you're probably seeing her in a book."

Now that's a hard saying. I buttoned my pants and left the room.

"Oh Clyde——?"

I came back in and said, "I didn't realize the lady was such a dear friend of yours. But that makes it nice. That will make it easier for you to bear up."

"What do you mean?"

"I mean just that," I said. "If anything has really happened to poor Caddy—" I stopped to taste that word *poor*, "we're going to have to stick around. There's no way of getting out of that."

I left her there to think that over and walked through the house. I stood at the screen, looking out over the yard and the slanting, cool light dappling the hollow. A rooster crowed. The phone rang again.

"That you Muncy?"

"Yes—" I said.

"This Purdy. I'm here in the house. Second floor. Phone right here on the landing. Another phone in her room, guess she had phones all over the place."

"Well, what happened?" I said.

"Passed out in her sleep. Only way to do it, Doc says."

"Caddy's dead?" I said.

"You can bank on that," he said. I felt a certain excitement in his voice. "She's dead all right," he repeated, "you can bank on that."

"I'll tell Bud immediately," I said. "I suppose the Doc is going ahead?"

"We're going ahead, Captain—" he said, "Yes siree——"

"Well, thanks for calling—" I said. "We'll be right over."

"If you want to get me, Captain—" he said, "just ring any phone in the house. Phone right here before me is 711. Just ring that."

"O-kay—" I said, "we'll be right over," and as I put the receiver down I saw Bud, pulling on his pants, in front of the garage. When he looked up I saw one eye was swollen shut with mosquito bites. His ankles were raw where he had been scratching, and his right hand began to grope again, absently.

[114]

"Oh Bud—" I said, and crossed the room to the screen. He came to the door, peering up at me with one eye. "Mr. Purdy just called," I said.

"Yeah—?" he said, and I saw that he was ready.

"Caddy died in her sleep—" I said, pronouncing her name in a friendly fashion, "and both Purdy and the Doc are over at the house."

"What's that—?" called Nellie.

"Mrs. Hibbard—" Bud began, then he turned and said, "Well, I guess she's dead." The cheesecloth at the front of the garage swung back and there was Nellie, both eyes sealed shut. She put her hands to her face and said, "Didn't I tell you, Bud?"

"Yeah, I guess you did," said Bud, and looked down at his bitten feet. Then he looked up and said, "Well, what does that mean?"

"One thing it means," Nellie said, "is that we're moving out of this house." Then she lay back and said, "but I suppose there's other things first."

"It's going to be a long day," said Bud. "Guess we better eat."

In the middle of breakfast the phone rang again.

"Go ahead," said Bud, "you take it. You know what's going on." I took it and heard Mr. Purdy clear his throat.

"That you Captain?"

"Yes—" I said.

"This Purdy."

"How are things, Purdy?" I said.

"Doc asked me to find out if you people had any objection to Ralph Moody?"

"Not off hand—" I said. "Who is he?"

"Moody's Funeral Parlor," said Purdy.

"Oh—" I said, "hold on a minute."

"Right, Captain," he said.

I looked across the table at Bud, and said, "He wants to know what you think of Ralph Moody. If you think Moody's Funeral Parlor is o-kay?"

"They took care of Dad—" said Bud. "Did a nice job."

"Some people go to Lincoln," Nellie said. "You get nicer service—when I stop and think of Mother——"

"Don't forget you pay for it," said Bud.

"Is there any other?" I said.

Bud took a drink of coffee, then said, "Local people ought to give local men their business."

"What a way to talk, as if it's business—" said Nellie.

"Ralph's been here forty years," said Bud, "thirty of them because business is business."

"What would she think about it?" my wife said.

"*She*—?" said Nellie. "Oh heavens. Who wants to think about that? It's all right to bring it up, if you want to, but I'm not going to *think* about it."

"I got the old man here on the phone," I said. "Is it o-kay if I tell him Moody?"

"Go ahead," said Bud, "tell him."

I picked up the phone and said, "You there Purdy?"

"Here, Captain!" he said. I thought I heard his heels clicking.

"Moody seems to be all right," I said. "How is everything going?"

"Fine—just fine." He cleared his throat and said, "She's on her way down now."

[116]

"Already?" I said.

"Remember this is summer—hot weather."

"Oh, sure—" I said, and felt my head nodding.

"In July—" he began, then thought better of it. "You coming over?"

"We'll be right over, just getting a bite of breakfast."

"That's fine, Captain," he said. "You'll need it."

"You keep us posted—Chief," I said.

"Right, Captain," he said, then— "Right now I'm calling from the parlor. Phone down here too. Cooler down here. Coolest part of the house."

"How is Aunt Angie?" I said.

"She's fine." Then he said, "You people like me to handle the communication?"

I turned to Bud and said, "What about Aunt Angie? You want Purdy to handle it?"

"Hadn't you better do that?" Nellie said. "No Purdy has ever been a Hibbard—"

"He knows her," said Bud. "He knows how to handle her. Just like her to not believe a word I said."

"You go ahead and handle it, Chief," I said, "your own way."

"O-keydokey, Captain." I stood there, and heard his phone go down.

"Is this Purdy an old fool?" said my wife. "The two of you sound like a couple of kids?"

"He's an old man," said Bud. "In his seventies, I guess."

"I get the feeling," I said, "that this is quite an event for him. That he's been waiting for it a good many years."

"A good many people have," said Nellie, "and anybody can tell you Nellie Hibbard is one."

"She's as much as told some people," said Bud, "that we could have it when she was gone. But she didn't want us in it while she was around."

"That whole place to herself, with thousands lookin' for homes."

My wife opened her mouth— "Another piece of toast, Honey?" I said.

"I wonder what she'll do with that old electric?" said Bud. "Sat there in the garage, now, ten-fifteen years."

"Well, you don't want it," Nellie said.

"When I think of all those batteries—" said Bud. He shook his head. "You ever see her in that old electric?"

I nodded.

"Like a rubber-tired buggy," said Nellie, "you couldn't hear it creep up on you. There she was, like a bird in a cage. Real flowers in the vases on the door."

"There isn't anyone she'd give it to?"

"There was a woman, a seamstress—" Nellie said, "who came twice a year and lived in the house. Sewed in the house. They used to ride in it afternoons."

"Haven't seen her for ten or twelve years," said Bud.

"Came from St. Louis. Brought the new fashions out. When you saw them together you knew it was a new dress or a new jacket."

The phone rang again.

"You take it," said Bud. I took it.

"That you Captain?"

"Me," I said.

"Turns out we got another little problem. Seems Moody's got the Clay twins, two of 'em, and Mrs. Lorbeer. She came in first. She died last but I guess they got her over there first."

"I see—" I said.

"Both the Doc and me got to thinkin'," he said, "got to thinkin' that the place to lie out is right here. As Doc just said, where'd you find as nice a funeral parlor as this? Clean as a whistle an' cool. Important thing is it's cool."

"Hmmmmm—" I said.

"In case you folks think it's all right what we're goin' to do is to get her fixed up—you know, fix her up right here—'fore the news spreads all over the place. 'Fore we do that, you got to pick the box. Instead of comin' here, first thing to do is go by Moody's an' pick out a box, as the right sort of box is the next thing she needs. Mr. Moody called to say he'll be on hand to help you pick it out. Doc thinks the right place for the box is over here—I'm callin' from the first floor, over near the fireplace—room with the fireplace is big enough for people to file in, file out. You'd have to go to Lincoln for a nicer set up, Doc says."

"Hold it a second, Captain," I said.

"I'm Chief," he said, "you're Captain."

"Hold it, Chief," I said.

"O-kay Captain," he said, and I put the phone in my lap.

"Purdy says the Moody place is a little overcrowded, and that Doc suggests we use her own house. Says he thinks the house is the best place anyhow."

"Why, you know," Nellie said, "it *is* like a Funeral Home."

"It's dark enough," said Bud.

"And it's pretty cool," I said.

"What you think?" said Bud.

"This is a local problem," I said, "I'm just a city-boy."

"It's certainly every bit as good looking as Moody's." Nellie closed her other eye. "There's a slate roof."

"Hello—" I said to Purdy, "well, they seem to think it's o-kay."

"You'd have to go to Omaha—" he went on, "to find anything like it. Caddy had class—" he added, as an afterthought.

"You and Doc go right ahead. How is Aunt Angie?"

"Haven't got over there yet. To get around to her I have to leave the house, right here in front, and go around in back. People'll wonder what the devil I'm doin' in here."

"I see——"

"All depends on whether you want it to get out or not."

"What's that?" I said.

"The news, Captain——"

"Oh—" I said, "Oh yes."

"When that gets out we're going to have some people on our hands."

"You think so?"

"If I'm any judge, everybody in town is going to want a good look at her."

"Hmmmm—" I said.

"And I don't mean just the ladies," he said.

"Well, many thinks, Cap——"

"Chief—" he said. "I'm Chief—you're the Captain."

"We're just about to start over," I said. "We'll go right down to Moody's."

"When you get over here, Captain," he said, "suppose you use the door at the side." Then he said. "Oh Captain——"

"Yes—?"

"Wonder you could stop by Mabel's an' pick me up a cup of coffee, roll of some kind?"

"Why sure——"

"Not a thing in here to eat. Don't know what she lived on. Maybe she starved to death." I didn't say anything. "But the house is full of flowers—how'd she do that?"

"You got me, Chief—" I said, then heard the footsteps of someone behind him.

"Well, I got to lend a hand here, Captain—" he said, and hung up.

"These aren't toll calls, are they?" said my wife.

Nellie shook her head.

"Where we stand now?" said Bud.

"First we go by Moody's," I said, "where we pick out a box, a coffin, as he says they're going to need the coffin right away."

"Something simple," said Nellie, "we've got no money to bury in the ground."

"There'll be money for that all right," said Bud.

"You don't know a thing about it. We thought there'd be money for Mother. Was there? Not a cent. Four hundred dollars buried right in the ground."

"Maybe you'd like to come along an' pick it out?"

"An' who'd mind your children?"

"I would—" said my wife.

"You don't want to go along?"

"No thanks," she said. "No, no thank you." She put her lips together as she does at those times she's car-sick, or about to be photographed.

"Well, maybe I better then—" said Nellie. "I can't trust you men."

"You think you can see all right?" said Bud.

She had forgotten. She could see a bit now, but the lids were puffy, she looked a bit tight. As she turned to the mirror I could see that this would have been a hard morning, in more ways than one, if Caddy Hibbard hadn't altered it.

"Well, if you think you can see—" said Bud, and stood up.

As he stood there she said, "I suppose you thought you were going like *that?*" She looked at me and said, "Mr. Muncy here is just passing through, and everybody knows it, but you're not, you can just put on your blue serge suit." Bud started for the bedroom. "Besides, Caddy Hibbard's *your* relation," she said.

My wife got a clean shirt out of my bag, picked the lint from my pants. I walked out in the yard to wait for Bud, so Nellie could dress in the bedroom, and though it was early I saw that it was going to be hot. There was a blur at the end of the furrows in the plowed field. The morning color had faded from the sky. A dry wind, neither hot nor cold, blew through the door of the garage and the bushes of lilacs, but no particular odor, good or bad, got to me. Had I read somewhere that the dust was coming back?

"O-kay—" said Bud, and stepped out on the porch to button up his pants. At first glance I thought the blue serge suit was the one I had seen twenty years ago, when Bud, and forty other serge suits, had graduated from High School. It was still tight in the shoulders, the ankles, and the crotch. A man in a blue serge suit like this, of the vintage I am describing, affects me quite a bit like the rustling of papers on a Sunday afternoon. It takes me back a good deal farther than I care to go. Back to a suit of my own, just like it, and the number of times I had to stand, with my face in her hair, while my step-mother picked the lint off of me. Bud's narrow shoulders were gray with dandruff, worn in rather than brushed off, and the knees of the pants were cocked, as if he stood about to jump. He turned to call to Nellie, waving his hand, and I saw that the coat, and the seat of the pants, had the waterproof shine of a streetcar conductor's uniform. I could see between his legs, which were slightly bowed, and as he turned and crossed the porch I recognized the gait, the cocky walk, that his father had. Nellie came out, dressed as she was in last year's photograph, on the piano, and I turned from the house as I once did from the idle summer windows, the fly-cluttered screens, and the time-less afternoons, suspended like a wick in a kerosene lamp. I was sweating a little, and stopped to wipe my face with my sleeve.

We drove by Mr. Swenson, the last of the Vikings, standing in the shadow of his sagging porch, a crooked stick in his hand which he raised in the air, waved to us. The creaking lawn swing was gone, and there was a fence across the front of the yard.

"You begin alone, and that's how you end up," Nellie said.

"Weren't there some boys, too?" I said.

"They like to farm their own way," said Bud. "They went to Aggie College. But you can't tell the old man anything."

"He's wondering right now," Nellie said, "just what

it is we're up to. This time of the morning, riding around just as nice as you please."

"He say he'd told anyone?" said Bud.

I shook my head. "He said he hadn't. He said that was why he was staying in the house."

"When Mother died," Nellie said, "in the next room, the closet between us, I'd swear the people in Butler county knew it first."

"You watch," Bud said, "if somebody don't bring up a barking dog. How some dog or other woke him up. Barking."

"Well, there *was* a dog," said Nellie, "about three o'clock."

"I don't know why a dog should care," said Bud. "But if they cared I suppose they might bark."

"Moody—" I said. "His place still where it used to be?"

"Behind the Lyric," said Bud, and I took the next turn, went around the firehouse, and drew up in the shade facing an iron hitching post. A Neon sign stood in the yard before the Moody house. A room had been added at the rear, with a porch like a railroad platform, and there were two crated coffins near the door. Houses of this kind, all over the country, were seeing it through as Funeral Parlors, or the haunted center of a sprawling used-car lot. People had to die, and they had to have a car.

"Should I leave the car here?" I said.

"You got an out of town license," said Bud. "If we get right out, you might as well pull up an' park."

"You want me along?" I said.

"You better come along," said Bud. I parked the car in what I thought was a casual manner, and shut the door without slamming it. Before I reached the walk, however, or the Neon sign on posts in the yard, the front door opened and a woman beckoned to us. She held a handkerchief in her hand, which she alternately shook out and then squeezed, or pressed like a wad of cotton to two spots on her face. The moist, gill-like pouches under her wide eyes. This pressure seemed to release further moisture which brightened her eyes, like a spray, then gathered like tears which had to be lightly sopped up. She held open the screen and as we stepped inside and the door closed behind us, two musical chimes, one near and one far, echoed in the hall. At the same time fluorescent lights blinked on, like shells bursting in advance of the explosion, and I saw that Nellie's face, once tipsy red, was now old rose. Also Bud. We all looked very well, indeed.

Stepping from behind me, the woman said— "You're Mr. Hibbard?"

"I'm Mr. Muncy," I said. "This is Mr. and Mrs. Hibbard," and I turned to face Nellie and Bud.

"I'm Mrs. Dauber—" she said, in a hushed voice, her head forward, so that the peppermint flavor of her mouthwash got over to me. "Mrs. Dau-burr—Mrs. Moody's assistant—Mrs. Moody just called me to say that you were on your way here, that I should be expecting you."

"Doctor Sprague said we'd need a coffin of some kind," said Bud.

"Let me get Mr. Moody," she said. "He has the coffins, I have the flowers—" and she went off, careful to keep her heels on the rug. On the wall facing me, newly plastered, was an English print showing a coach and four, hounded by dogs, racing through the English countryside. The title of the print was *Carrying the Mail to Calais*.

"What about flowers?" said Bud. "I suppose we'll have to have some flowers."

"People give them," said Nellie, "don't they?"

"She didn't have a friend in the world," said Bud. "Not a friend. Who you think is going to give her flowers?"

In the adjoining room, signaling his arrival, Mr. Moody cleared his throat, scraped his feet on the rug, then came soberly forward.

"It's a great loss for us all," he said to me, and shook my hand.

"I'm Mr. Muncy—" I said, and then heard myself say, "I'm just passing through, on my way east." Mr. Moody was shaking hands with Bud.

"Didn't I bury your father?" he said.

"Yes sir," said Bud. "Nine years ago."

"A fine service," said Mr. Moody. "I remember it."

Making certain allowances for the word—and the man who stood there, with his heels together—Mr. Moody struck me as an honest, even a forthright man. Dying was a sad business, so make the best of it. Put in the rose colored lights to soften the women, the thick beige carpets to silence the men, and an air of sober rightness to relieve all concerned. We were born and we died. Make the best of it.

Through the wide sliding doors, now thrown open, and over the fireplace with the cast-iron log, was the portrait of the old man I had seen on the porch as a boy. Or driving his fine team of county-fair mares along the tracks. A big man, sometimes wearing spurs, who had been one of the first to tell me—in a fine hearty voice—that virtue was its own reward. That I should go about my business and keep my bowels clean. And this new Moody, a little smaller in scale, was his son. The world had changed, and the Moodys changed with the world. There was nothing in this life, nor in this new world, to explain the mystery he had chosen to deal with, so the least that he, a Moody, could do, was to make it tolerable. A new look, that is, for the old Dead Wagon. If this look was not to my taste, I could see that it did very well for Nellie, supporting her like a hand at her elbow, one on which she could lean. She gazed at Mr. Moody through her new oriental eyes. The puffed lids gave her a look of grief, a night of turmoil to say the least, and now that she looked her worst I began to see the best in her. Call it pluck. But this kind of pluck is a way of life. This new world—the one Nellie had to live in—was always there like a great bottle of insects, ready to break into her house, or pour through a new crack in her screen. Her hand was always reaching for the missing swatter, or the leaking Flit machine. This world was hell, to put it mildly, and the stiff upper lip, the lint on the blue serge, was not a pretty thing but it made life possible. To make it tolerable was Mr. Moody's problem. As it must to all men *it* had come to Caddy Hibbard, and now that *it* had she would have to be buried. All right. Make the best of it.

"Mrs. Dauber was saying—" Mr. Moody began.

"Doctor Sprague—" Nellie said, in a voice that seemed to come from behind her, but Mr. Moody, his hand raised, gently cut her off. He understood. He saw the picture, so to speak, every inch of it. Taking Nellie by the arm, as one guides the blind across the intersection, he walked before us toward the end of the hall. There he opened a door, going down, and as we entered the lights came on.

The vault room—as Mr. Moody described it, and which we saw in three directions from the landing—was the basement of the old Moody house. Arranged about the floor, from corner to corner, were a dozen or so caskets, like gift boxes, or freshly made hospital beds. They ranged from wood painted to look like metal, and metal treated to look like wood, to one made of wood, very simply, and one made of metal like a safety vault. And there was something to be said for coming *down* stairs to witness this. We were in the world below, and it was inhabited.

"Holy smoke—" said Bud, then getting a grip on himself, "I never seen so many of them—you do a big business?"

"Wherever people are—" said Mr. Moody, "they have to die. Then you've got people dead." He had said this many times, too many, perhaps, but he still believed it. Every word of it. He spoke the lines like a fellow mortal, soon doomed himself, but with the consolation that he was making the best of a sorry circumstance. Other men didn't know what lay ahead of them. Mr. Moody did.

"What we have in mind—" said Nellie, stepping down on the level with the caskets, "is something simple. We just can't afford anything else."

"I buried my father in a thirty-dollar box," Mr. Moody said. We all turned to him and he said, "The same box is now sixty, and that is the one I have in mind for myself."

"Well, now—" said Bud, and looked at Mr. Moody with a new understanding. "Well, now that sounds sensible to me."

"I have these things," said Mr. Moody, "because most people insist on them. I am a business man. I have to sell the people what they want."

"They really want this stuff?" said Bud, and nodded at the one he was facing. It looked something like a piece of hardwood linoleum.

"Speaking generally—" Mr. Moody said, and opened the lower button of his vest, "—ladies buy the caskets, and they usually want something nice. They don't want the rain, so forth, to get in touch with the loved one."

"How does it go now—" said Bud, "Dust we are to dust returneth——?"

"That's how it goes," said Mr. Moody, "but by and large most people don't like it. They admit it, but they don't want to see it. Put it that way. They want to keep the bugs out, I suppose, while they're around."

"I don't mind the dust idea—" said Bud.

"As I say," said Mr. Moody, "I've instructed my wife —but I've no guarantee that she will follow my Will. I've seen some very sensible people ignore the Will."

"You got one of these pine ones down here?" said Bud.

"I've been asked not to keep them in here," said Mr. Moody. "People find it too depressing, I guess, just to look at them."

"But you've got one?" said Bud.

"Oh yes. We always have them. The state buys them, you know, for the indigent and the poor."

"You know, I've often wondered about that," said Bud.

"Well, that's how it is," said Mr. Moody.

"You mean there's no difference," Nellie said, "between the pine box for Mrs. Hibbard, and the pine box for the poorhouse—so to speak."

"They're all just pine boxes," said Mr. Moody, and put out his hands, then dropped one hand and outlined an oblong pine box on the air. Thus and so. He buttoned the lower button once more.

"Now I don't know as I like that so much—" said Nellie.

"Another thing you might think of," said Mr. Moody, "is the plot and the grave itself. When the pine box rots, as it must, the grave of course sinks. In a family plot this sometimes offers certain difficulties."

"I've seen them," said Nellie, "and they're simply awful. I always wondered what it was that made them."

"Well, that's it. When the box decays, the grave—sinks."

"That isn't such a good idea," said Bud, "for a fact."

"You can put in a concrete vault," said Mr. Moody, "but most people think it's silly to save the box if it isn't worth anything."

"That makes sense," Nellie said. Bud agreed.

"The last thing—" said Mr. Moody, "or perhaps the first, depending on the type of service—is the viewing, if and where that is to take place. A pine box is hardly suitable in some instances."

"You mean we're in the coffin," said Nellie, "at the time?"

Mr. Moody nodded, gravely.

"Where is the viewing to be, Mrs. Hibbard?" he said.

"At her home," said Nellie.

Perceptibly, Mr. Moody flinched. He blinked several times, once more released the lower button of his vest.

"If the viewing is to be—" he said, "in the residence of Mrs. Caddy Hibbard, I'm inclined to recommend something other than a simple pine box." He looked around. "Something a little more appropriate," he said.

"We can't have a *pine* box," Nellie said. "I can see that. Mr. Moody—what would you suggest?"

"If you folks will pardon me," I said, "I just remembered that I have an errand. Mr. Purdy. He's waiting for his coffee and roll."

"This can be very exhausting," said Mr. Moody, "even though you don't feel like it, you should eat. Fainting, nausea, so forth, are often the result of not eating."

"Well, I'd better take care of Mr. Purdy," I said.

"You go ahead—" said Bud. "When I'm through here we'll try to get over. It's only five blocks. Little walk will do us good."

"O-kay—" I said, and came to the top of the stairs. As I opened the door I could hear Mrs. Dauber—and see her in the oval mirror in the hall—speaking to several elderly ladies at the door. The screen was closed. She did not offer to let them in. On the landing beside me was a small chair, a table with a nightlamp and a phone, and under the sheet of glass on the table were several notes and cards. *Take Notice* was written across the top of one of them. This clipping was captioned—THE PLEASE OMIT FLOWERS MOVEMENT—the unimportant details had been cut away, but the caption, and the critical passage, had been glued to a card. Key words and phrases were also underlined in red.

One director (name on file) with only two "omit notices" in two years, said his successfull method went like this: He tells bereaved a funeral piece doesn't mean just bouquet or spray of flowers: it means employment—

jobs—for the American Way of Life. Proved convincing except in two cases mentioned. If "omit flowers" movement keeps on might lead to cutting down on funeral service, use of better caskets, encourage simple burials. Might lead to cremation etc. All Directors please take notice and cooperate.

"You like the operator?" said Mr. Moody. He was peering at me through the basement stairs. They were gathered at the wood-into-metal division of the casket art.

"Just an address—" I said, "I was just looking up an address," and wrote the words "omit flowers" on the fringe of the telephone pad. I tore this sheet off, folded it, smiled at Mr. Moody, then stepped briskly into the hall. Mrs. Dauber was not at the door. The chimes rang as I opened it, and the far one followed me out on the porch, to the edge of the lawn where Mrs. Dauber was cutting fresh flowers. There was no sun in the shady yard but she wore a blue bonnet, with a trailing ribbon, and in her right hand she held a small pair of trimming shears. Something in the way she stood, as if in balance, and in the way she held the shears, chirping like a cricket, made me think of Miss Caddy, a primrose among the flowering corn. Perhaps Mrs. Dauber, all of these years, had wanted a flowering garden that she could stand in, a pair of shears dangling from the yellow ribbon about her throat. A bonnet shading her face, her moist eyes, and of an evening apt to be mistaken for Miss Caddy Hibbard, and useless women of that ilk. A delicate thing—as Clinton Hibbard described her—subject to frightful afternoon headaches brought on by exertion, physical exertion, of any kind. Better tell the customer a funeral piece doesn't mean just a bouquet, or a spray of flowers—tell him it means employment, jobs, for one American Way of Life. The dying one. The blue bonnet in the flowering corn.

Mrs. Dauber turned, nearly falling, to offer me a flower —would I like it?

"Why—yes," I said, but it was necessary for me to go and get it, to see how fresh it was, to remark how difficult cutting one simple flower can be. "Mrs. Muncy loves flowers," I said, and in the shadow of her bonnet I saw her yellow teeth, and the red gill-like rims of her moist eyes. "I'll run this right out to her," I said, and carried it erect, on its long prickly stem, across the yard and between the hitching posts, got into the car. There I had to make a shift, to reach the ignition, and as she was still watching me, I put the prickly stem of the flower between my teeth. In this fashion, a little abruptly, I drove away. Four or five blocks west I turned to the right, put the flower in the snap lid on the ash tray, and came back along the tracks toward Mabel's Lunch. The woman who had made my ice coffee was sweeping the walk.

"We been wondering where you was," she said, and took one hand from the broom to snap a shoulder strap, then point through the door. "Mabel's inside. Mr. Purdy called an hour ago."

Mabel was inside, on the first stool at the far end. A cup of coffee with a spoon in it sat in front of her. She took a swallow of the coffee, using her thumb to keep the spoon handle out of her eye, then she wiped her mouth with the back of her wrist.

"You boys want your coffee black or white?" she said.

"How does Mr. Purdy like it?" I said.

"He likes it hot," said Mabel. "Outside of that I'd say coffee is coffee for him."

"Say we take it black," I said, "with a little cream on the side."

She got up from the stool and took a quart milk bottle from the shelf beneath the counter, put a knife in the bottle, let the coffee dribble over it. "You got a place you can heat it up?"

"No—" I said. She took the knife out, wiped the blade on her haunch, put the stopper in.

"Never tastes as good as it smells—does it?"

"I guess nothing does."

"Oh, cheese does," she said. She took a paper bag from beneath the counter and put two rolls in it, rolled the bag up.

"How much do I owe you?"

"Owe me?" she said. "Don't we all have our troubles, don't we now?"

"Yes, I guess we do——"

"We can't do much but we can all do something. We can do a little bit."

"You're right there, all right," I said, and picked up the bag, put my hand on the bottle.

"I could've put ice in that bottle," she said, "but Mr. Purdy likes it hot. You know what I mean?"

"I know what you mean," I said. I had my hand on the door when she said—

"When he called me I said, I suppose you like it hot. What you mean like it hot? he said. I suppose you don't know Mr. Muncy likes it cold, with ice in it, I said." She waited.

"What did he say to that?" I said.

"Well, I suppose coffee is coffee, he said, if you got a cigar to go along with it." She looked at the case and said, "Is the King Edwards the ones I got out on top?"

As I turned down Pioneer Ave. I could see a Ford Coupe, Doc Sprague's car, drawn up in the ditch grass at the side of the house. I parked a half block to the east, near the empty lot. There was a short-cut across the lot and through Uncle Billie's garden of weeds, the tomato plants gone, but most of the poles still up. The clothesline sagged between the back of the house and the sheds. I stopped in the alley, the bottle in my hand, to see if the coast was clear, as there was a stretch of open lawn between me and the house. The door at the side stood open an inch or two. I headed for it, along the clothesline, but near the middle of the yard I heard the racket on the other side of the house. Aunt Angie and her birdbox again. Then it stopped, and I cocked my head to a whine, like that of an insect, but it was a lawn mower several blocks away. Cutting grass near the trees. Short whines, like a siren, then quiet again. I walked to the side door, stepped in, and was about to call out the old man's name, when I saw him—or thought I saw him—in the adjoining room. He was seated in a large platform rocker, that is, he had been seated, until he had slipped, as it was too much of a chair for a man to sit in, and let himself go. The angle was wrong, for one thing, and the wide, spring-cushioned arms spread a seat for lovers, young lovers, not an old one. The chair was covered with velvet, of an olive green, with strips of yellow lace pinned to the arms, and several inches above his head, above his hat, a crocheted antimacassar.

Platform rockers being what they are, Mr. Purdy looked sick, but he was there, and a leather-bound volume of *The Ladies' Floral Cabinet* was open in his lap. His shoes were off, placed to one side, and his faded red socks, with the white heel patches, were toes up on the polar bear rug. An old man at ease in an empty house—dozing, as he should be—except for the tilt of the summer straw hat on his head. It had not been tipped there, or bumped there, casually. This particular tilt was that of a man who buttons his vest, facing the mirror, tilts the straw hat, then steps back to consider himself. In my father's house, for one year, my uncle wore his hat like that from room to room, but he was careful to correct the angle on leaving the porch. The man in the heart, not the man in the street. For a good many years this man Purdy had lived right across the street from Miss Caddy Hibbard, and perhaps, now and then, he had stood at the open screen. He had seen the fur rug, and the platform rocker with the velvet seat. He had seen himself, Lemuel T. Purdy, seated there. At his ease with his shoes off, dozing, a leather-bound volume in his lap, and a lady with fingerless gloves playing snatches on the baby grand. Perhaps as fine a woman as Miss Caddy Hibbard, who needed help. And then came the day, as he knew it would, when he stood in the house, facing himself and the rocker, and before sitting down his hands came up, gave a tilt to his hat.

When I stepped into the hall this picture blurred—it was in the mirror on the back of the door—and Mr. Purdy was in the room across the hall. I let it close, a little sharply, and the old man sat up, reaching blindly for his

[136]

shoes—then he put down his shoes to raise both hands to his straw. He set it straight—then he decided to take it off. He put it in his lap, then from his lap to the floor.

"That you, Captain?" he called, and fumbled with his shoes.

"It's me—" I said, and walked down the hall, looked in at him. He had the book open; he closed it on his finger, marking the place.

"Thought I might as well rest a bit, Captain—" he said. "It's going to be a long day." I passed him the paper bag of rolls, put the bottle of coffee on the floor. "Why don't I get a couple of cups—" he said, "both have some?"

"Fine—" I said.

He pushed up from the chair, walked directly to a glass cupboard, which he opened with a key from the ledge over the sideboard, and took out two demitasse cups, two matching saucers. "Like the little ones," he said, "makes you think you're getting more." Coming back into the light he passed me a cup. "Nice stuff," he said.

"Yes, that's pretty nice stuff," I said. The inside of the cup was covered with gold leaf. A film discolored the porcelain shell, but Mr. Purdy took out his hanky, blew on the cup, then rubbed it with his finger. That didn't work. He dipped his finger in the coffee. That did.

"Never been used—anyhow, for thirty years," he said. He filled both cups, seated himself, took a sip of the coffee. "Well—" he said, "picture old Purdy doing this!" He wagged his head. He had waited a long time. "When the house was used—" he went on, "twenty-five, thirty years ago, the Missus—Caddy—used to ask me over to help clean things up. Suppose you noticed how I knew where these things were?" I nodded. "Guess I'm the only man that did. Don't think she knew herself." He fumbled for a roll in the paper bag, took a bite out of it. "When the time comes, Captain—" he said, "your little old Purdy is the only one—" he stopped to swallow, "who's goin' to know a few things. Made it a point. Thirty years now. S'why I remember it."

"That will be a great help, all right," I said, and looked around at the room. There was not much light—the shutters spread it out on the floor, in a bright, striped pattern —but I could see the grand piano, with the faded sheet music curling on the stand. A Paisley shawl was draped gracefully over the back. Several small chairs, with delicate legs, elaborate needlepoint on seat and back cushions, were arranged in semicircle as if for students, or visiting swains. The polar bear, with his wax red mouth, peered out from beneath.

"See them little chairs?" I nodded. "For two, three years—in the war, I think—young fellows from Lincoln come to play the violin. The big an' little violins. Played all together, you know. At the same time." He stopped to let that sink in. "Came down together, in a red car, drove back the same night."

"Did Clint like music?" I said.

"Don't think he did. Anyhow, he never sat around here much. Think he tolerated it more than he liked it. He was a busy man."

"When did he die?" I said.

"Thirties—" said Purdy, "early thirties. Don't know if you noticed, but a lot of busy people died about then."

"Something to do with money?"

He poured himself another cup of the coffee. "Young man," he said, "you think the only thing that kills a man is money?" He swallowed the coffee, like a whiskey, drew his sleeve across his face. He put the cup on the floor and drummed his fingers on the crown of his straw.

"How is everything going," I said. "All right?"

"You mean Caddy?" I nodded. "Just fine and dandy —you want to take a look?"

"No thanks—" I said.

"Well, she looks just fine." He wiped his forehead again and said, "You feel warm in here?"

"It's a little bit still," I said.

"Yes, I suppose it is. I suppose that makes it a little warm." He fanned his face with his straw and said, "Times before, I was just in and out. Seemed cooler." He looked at the shuttered windows. "Don't want to fool around with them just yet."

"She's going to be upstairs?" I said.

"No, down here. When they get her finished." He looked behind the piano and said, "Doc thinks over there. File them in an' around the piano, file them out again. It's in here everybody used to see her, right place for her."

"It was heart, I suppose—" I said.

"If that's what you want to call it. Doc said she run down—like that clock over there, tick-tock, tick-tock." He leaned over for another bun. "Doc says there's people you have to wind up. Then there's Aunt Angie—people who never run down."

"You tell her?" I said.

"Haven't got around to it." He let his upper plate drop and wiped the trough clean with the tip of his finger, put the dough into his mouth again.

"Don't you think she ought to be told?"

He chewed on the bun. "Thought so this morning. More I let it go, more I think about it, more I don't know."

"You think she knows?"

"I don't know what I think—Captain," he said. I sat back, but the chair wasn't comfortable. There were no other chairs in the room but the little ones, with the padded seats, the platform rocker, and the piano bench. I pulled the bench over near the light, sat on it.

"What did they all sit on," I said, "when I was a boy?"

"Funny thing—" he said, "think I used to wonder about that. Guess they sat on the stairs—" he nodded toward the broad flight of stairs back in the shadows, "or they sat in the swings, the hammocks, out on the porch. Think I remember she sat on the stairs herself. Like a kid. Knees drawn up, you know. Something she liked about it."

I looked at the stairs, the broad landing, the wide sweep to the second floor, and I thought I could see the tier on tier of lovely girls and fresh young men, napkins on their knees, balancing a saucer or a demitasse. Through the delicate rungs of the bannister they had a view of the room, the wide hallway, and the lovely lady, or ladies, seated at the baby grand. The young man bending low, his brow furrowed, tuning his violin.

"You was never inside here, Captain?"

"Just in the kitchen," I said. "Bud and I were just kids —not old enough for stuff like this." I turned to look at the piano, the semicircle of chairs.

"Weren't them lanterns the prettiest thing you ever seen?" Mr. Purdy leaned forward to peer through the shutters, as if they were there. "Don't know how they looked from here—was never in here when they was lit

[140]

up—but they were pretty as a grass fire from across the street." He wagged his head. "My room was right there on the corner, right at the front."

"It must have been a little noisy, too," I said.

"Oh pshaw—" he said, "you don't mind." He smiled and lidded his eyes. "I guess I wasn't so old myself." He poured another coffee and said, "Captain—you ever think what it's like to live in a town—" he stopped to think what he was saying, "to live—" he said, "right across the street there for forty-five years?"

"You mean," I said, "right across the street from a house like this?"

"Right across—" he said, "from a woman like Caddy." He finished the coffee, wiped his fingers on the top of the bag. "Right across—" he repeated, and lay back, closing his eyes.

No, I hadn't thought about what that was like. I thought about it now.. Many men knew thoughts like that.

My Uncle Dwight, an impulsive man, lived for nearly twenty years just a block down the street, just a sound of the rocker away from the woman in his life. Another man's wife. He passed this man's house twice a day. This woman often sat on the porch with the other man's children in her lap, and the other man's voice, or one of his boys, calling her name. Her own voice could be heard in our yard, answering him. For maybe twenty-five years this woman sat in the swing from where she could see my Uncle Dwight, and he sat on the steps, or weeded dandelions, so that he could see her. What had come of it? One winter day the woman died.

"That was the year—" Purdy said, as if he knew what

I had been thinking, "that Mr. Clinton Hibbard, Uncle Billie's son, laid the foundation for a fine new home." He tapped the floor with his foot. "This one. Spring nineteen-nine. Year later Caddy—Mrs. Hibbard—came out here to live in it. It was Clinton who asked me if I wouldn't lend a hand around the house."

I got up and walked to the shutters in the bay, peered out at the yard. On the porch across the street, leaning on her broom, a woman gazed directly at the Hibbard house. At the second floor where the blinds were drawn, Miss Caddy's room.

"That give you the picture?" Purdy said.

"Yes, that's the picture all right," I said.

"Feels—" he said, looking around the room, "as if I was born and raised in it—you know what I mean?" I turned from the window and he said, "You might even say that I lived over here—" he patted the arm of the chair, "more than I lived over there." He turned as if looking across the street. As he did, he seemed to see something as he stooped over, peered through a slit in the shutters. "Hmmmmm—" he said. "Well, Captain, just as I thought——"

I put my nose to the window on his left. A very large man, in a tight seersucker suit, was backing out of a Model A coupe. He stood in the ditch grass to pull down his coat, pull up his pants. As he did this he turned to glance, in what he considered a casual manner, at the wide empty yard, the shuttered house at the back of it. He removed his straw hat and studied the label, set it level on his head. Once more he tugged at his coat, which showed a tendency to climb, then leaned into the Ford

[142]

and reappeared with a long narrow box. As he came up the walk Purdy said, "Captain, you better take over. He'd never live to grow up if he opened that door, saw me standin' there."

"Me—?" I said.

"Nobody knows you from Adam," he said.

He tip-toed across the room to the chair, sliding his shoes around behind it, then he hurried behind the piano as the chimes rang.

As I walked to the door he said, "He'll think you're part of Moody's new outfit," then he ducked his head when I turned to look at him.

I had a little difficulty opening the door. Through the frosted glass, with the stenciled design, I could see the big fellow and the small box held before him in the manner of a bassoon. As the door creaked in, and before I could put my hands on the screen, he said— "Compliments of the First Methodist Church, Ma'am," then he excused himself, bowing, when he saw me.

"Thank you very much," I said, and took the box from his hands.

"We all feel this loss and your sorrow," he said, and held his stiff straw in such a manner that he could drum, with the fingers of both hands, on the lid.

"Thank you very kindly," I repeated, and looked at the card, attached to the box cord.

> The Lord Jesus Christ
> is with us in our
> Grief

When I glanced up I could see that he was relieved.

[143]

"The Lord really is, you know," he said.

"I'm sure of that," I said, a remark that seemed to mean a good deal to him. His face relaxed, he looked at the band in his hat.

"Some people don't know how to receive," he said, speaking to me now off the cuff, "they really don't, you know. It's a pleasure to deal with those who do."

"We're all very grateful," I said, "and we want to thank you."

"Thank *you*," he said, put on his hat, and backed from the porch. At a trot he went down the walk, through the ditch, to his car.

"You know—" Purdy said, over my shoulder, "I think both the Doc and me forgot about flowers. Plumb forgot 'em. Is the piano the place for 'em?" He took the box from my hands, walked into the front room. "You begin to see the picture, Captain—" he said, "Caddy back there, up against the fireplace, piano over here, covered with flowers and that sort of thing." He smiled at me. He saw the picture very well himself. "Basement's full of flower vases—" he went on, "when she was up they was all over the house." With the box, he walked down the hallway to the rear. From the dark he called—"You like to call your wife—or somebody? Think I told you we got phones —telephones all over the place." Then he opened the basement door, which creaked, and went down the stairs.

I sat down for a moment, then got up to answer another ring of the chimes. Through the frosted glass I saw two hats—ladies' hats. I opened the door and saw two ancient women, withered and fragile, holding between them a small basket containing flowers. They looked from one to the other, then one said— "We have come——"

"—to offer our sympathy," said the other. Whereupon they both nodded their heads, bowed to each other, then turned to me. I took the basket from their bony, bird-like hands. Small blue straws sat on their heads, which they cocked to one side, like worming robins, waiting for the victim to move again.

"Is there anything—" the first began.

"—that we can do?" answered the other.

"We would be very——"

"—happy."

"Very happy——"

"—indeed." They faced each other, nodding, then turned back to me.

"Thank you very much," I said, "but everything is under——"

"—control?"

"Yes—" I said, "everything is under control."

"We would very much appreciate——"

"—the basket," said the second. "If it is all right—" she turned to the other.

"—we will call for it."

"I'll see that it is put aside," I said. They turned away, stepping down from the porch carefully, as if blindfolded, then idling down the walk on their stilt-stiff legs like moulting water birds. Out under the trees they paused to wheel slowly, sight down the walk, agree on what they saw, then debate on what direction to take. I could see that the lack of a basket was a hamper to them. A connection was broken. They had to establish it again.

[145]

"Minnie Mae and Becky—" Purdy said. "Well, I guess it's out, Captain. I guess it's all over." I turned to look at the flowers, the lilies, he had in a bowl. Water dripped from his hands on the floor. "From now on, Captain," he said, "your Uncle Dudley's goin' to have his hands full." Swinging the basket, I followed him across the room.

In his opinion the pie-ano belonged near the center of the floor. "As I see it, Captain—" he said, "we bring 'em in the door—" he made the proper gesture, "then we single file 'em around the pie-ano—then we shoo 'em upstairs."

"You going to run 'em *up* stairs?"

"Might as well, that's where they'll be. Besides, we got to shoo 'em somewhere. We'll never get 'em out." He looked around the room and said, "Take it from your Uncle Dudley, Captain, until the last light in this house is off, you'll never get 'em out." He looked pleased. "Don't you know how women are yet?"

"Well, maybe I don't."

"Well, your Uncle Dudley does," he said. I could see that he had waited, since morning, anyhow, for me to realize that he was my Uncle Dudley. Not the Chief, the Captain, or such stuff as that. He was my Uncle Dudley Hibbard, one of the Uncle Billie line. He faced the fireplace and said, "I see her lyin' about here." He stepped a foot to the left. "Don't want them gawkin' at her from the door. An' we got to keep 'em movin' or they'll stand an' count the beads on her party dress." He looked at me. "Told Moody to bring that box along on one of those wheel things, seen 'em in hospitals. All we got to do is push her in, push her out. We'll set her right here, file 'em in through the door an' to the right of the pie-ano, then to the left into the parlor or up the stairs. You can bet your life all of 'em who can will go up the stairs."

I let myself down on the platform rocker, tried to visualize it. It was not hard. That surprised me a little bit. I could see them on the stairs, Mabel and Lily, Lily with her hair like a soiled oil mop, Mabel with a lint sprinkled coat, the flap open at the front, like a tent. And on the broad landing Minnie Mae and Becky, like a pair of stuffed, mechanical birds, slowly craning their heads while they passed a sentence, like a piece of carding wool, back and forth between them. These stairs would be crowded, as from there, either on the wide turn or from the landing, one could reconsider, at a distance, what one had seen in the box. The narrow face of Caddy, more than ever, surely, like a goat. There would be a smudge of color, like the bloom on wax fruit, and the lidded eyes would be like a doll's, apt to rock open if something disturbed the weights in the head. But you would look, for perhaps you had never seen her face. Only the shadow, the sunken image you sometimes see at the bottom of a well, for the face of Caddy was always withdrawn into her flowering hats. Here in the box, at least, one could really look at her. As you would look at your childhood, or the best impression you had of yourself. I knew this as well as any man, and if I did not come for a look at Caddy it was because I knew it, because it privately scared me to death. For I knew that more had died, upstairs, than I had reckoned with. I had also died, and the gist of my life was to be born again.

The phone rang.

"You better get that, Captain—" Purdy said, "tell 'em you're from Moody's, the only man here."

I picked up the receiver. "That you Clyde? This is Mabel. Mabel's Lunch."

"Why hello, Mabel—" I said.

"It's past two—ain't it time you boys had somethin' to eat?"

"Is that Mabel—?" Purdy said, but as I nodded my head she was gone. There was a click in the phone.

"Awful sorry, Clyde—" another voice said, "this me, Irene. The operator."

"Hello Irene——"

"Bud Hibbard just called and asked me to getcha, and so I told Mabel she could wait for she can getcha at any time."

"I suppose that's right," I said.

"It's right around here," said Irene. "Well, here's Bud——"

"Hello—" said Bud. "This is Bud."

"Hello Bud—" I said.

"I'm going to try to run Nellie into Lincoln, Clyde, as her eyes don't look so good, but she's a hard one to doctor. She thinks all doctors do is cost you money—your wife like that?"

"Sure—" I said, "they're all like that."

"Is that Bud?" said Purdy, and took the phone from my hands. "This Purdy speakin'—" said Purdy. "Everything over here just hunky-dory, your ole Uncle Dudley's got the situation well in hand. Me and the Captain—" he said, waving his hand, "sittin' here like two clams at high tide." He put the phone down, turned to me and said— "All these Hibbards the fidgety type."

Mabel didn't get around to calling again, but she sent over a boy with four hamburgers, another quart of coffee, *iced*, and about half of a fresh peach pie. After the meal we had a smoke, as she had also sent along four King Edward cigars—without the bands, however, as she kept them for the kids.

"But you can tell a King Edward—" Purdy said, biting off the end, and I could see that he could. As we smoked, facing the pie-ano, and Purdy's idea of a flower arrangement, he began to speak of things, several things, that weighed on his mind. For a good many years, so it seemed, Mr. Purdy had been working on a little matter, an invention, of sorts, that would probably make him rich.

And what was that, I said.

A chick feeder—one the little fellows couldn't drown themselves in. He paused to let me get the full range of the thing. He took another cigar and lay back—something pretty hard to do in a platform rocker—but he coiled one arm behind his head, tipped his hat down low on his face. It made me realize that we had come—Mr. Purdy and I —quite a ways since morning. We were on a new level. We had something in common, so to speak. In one afternoon, somehow or other, accepting all the recognized timeworn barriers, we had reached a situation of considerable intimacy. In all of Junction, I realized, or the world at large for that matter, perhaps I alone knew of the foolproof Purdy Chick Feeder. Nothing but the war, and the metal shortage, had held him back.

"Well, it sounds like a real cinch," I said.

"They estimate—" the old man said, lidding his eyes to recall the figure, "that one out of ten people in this country have something to do with chicks. That's fourteen million—say we make it just ten to deal in round numbers. Ten million chick feeders say, at about three dollars a piece." He stopped to roll the tip of his King Edward between his lips. "Conservatively speaking, Captain—" he went on, "ought to clear a silver dollar on every feeder, taking care of production, outlying stocks and bonds, collateral, so forth——"

When he said stocks and bonds, collateral, etc., I turned my head to face the shuttered window, as I seemed to see my father, as well as hear him, seated across from me. Another great believer in the magical words, the Voodoo rites of stocks and bonds, the inner sanctum mysteries of something described as *collateral*. With collateral my father believed anything could be done. Collateral could make, or unmake, an American. If the green grocer has so many heads of lettuce which he sells for so and so many dollars, how much must the green grocer make to realize his collateral? How much the farmer to sell the green grocer? How much collateral to bamboozle an American?

"That sounds really great, Chief—" I said, using the words I used for my father, and the cheery, false voice —*that sounds really great, Dad*, I would say.

"Patents cost me sixty-nine fifty. Just for the patents. What you think of that?" He peered at me, his head wagging happily. "PURDY-FEEDER—now how you like that?"

"For the ladies—?" I said.

"Why I asked. Was wondering if you might think of that. Why I tried it out. Like to see, you know, how all kinds people react."

"Well, they might wonder," I said. "Some people take names like that pretty literal."

"Then there's NO-DROWNT—" he said. "How you like that?"

"That's a little abrupt."

"Way I felt myself. Don't want to scare 'em bug-eyed. Might decide not to have any chickens at all."

"Was it Bud—" I said, "who was tellin' me about your health powder?"

"PURDY-QWIK," he said. "It didn't go over so good." He pushed his hat back and said, "Take it from your Uncle Dudley, boy, don't try an' ever sell the American people powdered grass. They won't buy it. Nine out of ten of 'em would rather stay sick."

"Was the stuff any good?" I said.

"Taken it for years. Never had a bit of trouble. Swells up in the bowels, helps carry the soft stuff along." He looked at me. "You ever in your life hear of a constipated cow?" I shook my head. "Well, that's why, Captain—" he said.

The air—it was a little thick now, like the surface of water just over our heads—or perhaps it was thoughts of that cow, or cows, that made us drowsy. He tipped his hat low on his face again, crossed his hands in his lap. "It's going to be quite an evening, Captain—" he said, "what you say we take a little snooze?"

"You go right ahead, Chief—" I said, "I got some things I better do."

"Why'nt you phone? Phones handy all over the place."

"Think my wife's all alone out there," I said. "I better run along."

"You got to run off—?"

"I'll see if I can't get back," I said.

He puffed at his cigar, but it had gone out. He dropped the butt in the plastic thermos cap. "One little thing you might do, Captain—" he said. "On your way—on your way out."

"Sure—" I said, "anything."

He tried to sit up, but the chair was too much for him. "You want to give me a hand, Captain?" I gave him a hand. He sat there a moment, belching, his hands on his knees. "What I'd like you to do—" he said, and stopped there, to adjust his hat. As he put it on, level, I knew what he meant to say. "Thought you might—" he said, "on your way out just stop an' say a word to Aunt Angie." He looked down the hall. "You gotta go out, be right on your way." I didn't answer, and he said, "But of course if you don't want to——?"

"Why shouldn't I——?"

He wagged his head. "Well, you know how some people are—idea, I suppose, of bringin' up certain things."

"I know——"

"Just stop by an' let her know—that's all." He turned to the window and said, "You know, just so she'll know." As I stood up he added, "You can tell her through the window, the bird-box. You can tell her like that if you don't want to go in. Well, she's gone, Aunt Angie, you can say—you won't have to say much."

"O-kay," I said. "I'll take care of it."

"If I should start runnin' around right now—get in some kind of argument with her——"

"I understand," I said. "You leave it to me."

"I got plenty to worry about right here. Whole business tonight. Might have forty, fifty people here."

"Well, Captain—" I said, "I'll stop by and see you tonight."

"Now you do that. Bring your wife an' youngsters along. Women always enjoy it. Never knew a woman to turn it down."

"I'll see what she says———"

The phone rang, and he said— "You go ahead, I'll take over now, Captain—" and he tipped back his hat, picked up the phone.

"This Purdy, speaking. Ohhh Libby. Didn't recognize your voice. No, no, everything just fine. No, no, Mabel sent us up a nice little snack from town. Muncy—old friend of family. Knew her well." He covered the mouthpiece and said, "My cousin, Libby—curious, you know. Say, Libby—" he went on— "one thing you can do is get out my suit. No, black, satin on collar. Better brush it off. No, just figure I'll have to wear it over here tonight. Think so. Expect quite a turnout, quite a little crowd."

As I walked down the hall he winked his left eye, waved at me. I opened the side door, looking out on the garden, and saw moving along the walk, in a processional manner, five or six women, one bearing flowers. This lady wore a boa, a white plume in her hat, and was propped semi-upright by a whalebone corset, the umbrella-like tips sticking up along her back. Her front was somewhat wrinkled, but neither of her heavy arms would reach that far. Nor to her hat, which she reached for, absently, now and then. Near the front of the house they gathered around her, a huddle, a discussion of tactics, and before it broke up I let myself out, ran for the rear. Aunt Angie's door was propped ajar with a Monkey Ward catalogue.

Before I rapped she said, "Why don't you come in?" As I stepped in she said, "How long's it take you to learn that door's never locked?"

"Where I come from, Aunt Angie," I said, "a gentleman always knocks on a lady's doorway."

"Where you come from?" she said.

"Right here," I said.

"That's what I thought. People who don't know a hawk from a handsaw all come from here."

She was seated in her rocker, near the bird-box, with a mug on the floor beside her with a green-handled spoon and a wet bed of coffee grounds. A strip of new Afghan was in her lap, the long bone needles tucked into the ball of red yarn she was working on. The night before I hadn't had the time to notice her shoes, which she kept under her chair, but now she sat with her left leg crossed, the foot rocking. The single-button pump, with the button gone, dangled from her foot. The pointed heel was like the well chewed end of a cane.

"Lookee here—" she said, "where's that Purdy?"

"He's busy right now, Aunt Angie."

"If Purdy's busy, it's the first time in his life." I let that pass. "Well, I suppose you wouldn't know that," she said. She began to rock as she said, "Until he took to seein' me I don't know what he had to do. He reads nice. He reads so I can hear."

"You like me to read?"

"No, I don't. To hear you talk any poor body can tell what you read don't mean a thing."

"I don't know these people," I said.

"You need to tell me that?" She hmmmmphed. Then— "But I don't know as you missed so much."

[154]

At the front of the house the chimes rang. I turned my head.

"You hear that?"

"What?" I said.

"Now say—" she said, "what's goin' on in that house?"

"I don't know," I said. "Maybe somebody isn't well."

"Hmmmmmm——"

"Mr. Purdy tells me," I said, feeling around for an opening, "that the woman who lives up front is pretty sick. Pretty sick, he said. He told me the doctor was there last night."

"Purdy told you that?"

"That's what he told me."

"He'd like to live in such a fine house himself." Her brows arched. "You men are such fools," she said.

"Mr. Purdy said—" I went on, "that this woman was so sick that he wouldn't be at all surprised to hear the worst."

"And what could that be?"

"Well—" I said, then let it drop when she turned from me, abruptly, as if she heard another squirrel in the birdbox. She leaned forward, her elbows propped on her knees. I could see her reflection in the window, the slight movement of her lips, and the click of her plates that told me she was talking to herself. I stepped back, then forward when she said, "There it goes—there it goes."

"What Aunt Angie?" I said.

"There it goes—" she said, craning her head, "the Dead Wagon!"

I put my face to the window to see, nodded my head as if I saw it, near the corner, then said, "Well, maybe it's happened, maybe this is it." She kept her eyes to the hole in the bird-box, she did not look at my face. "Maybe Mr. Purdy was right," I said, "just as he said, maybe this is it." She still did nothing. "Well, I guess I better go and give him a hand." She remained right there, propped on her arms. She did not watch me leave. I went out in the yard, then cut around to see if the ladies had left the house, as Purdy would be glad to hear that I had broken the news. He was standing at the front of the hall, peering out through the frosted glass.

"Well Chief—" I said, walking toward him, "for once that Dead Wagon business fit the picture. This time that wagon came along at just the right time."

"How's that?" he said.

"The Dead Wagon," I repeated, "for once it came along at just the right time." He stared at me. I had the feeling he didn't see anything. "I was just beginning to wonder," I said, raising my voice a notch or two, "how to bring the subject up, when that damn wagon came along. Just as nice as you please. All I had to do was tell her it was probably stopping here. For the lady up front. She could figure out the rest."

"Got some more flowers—" he said, turning from me to wave at the piano. There were also flowers in a bowl near the window, lilies in the hall.

"That's fine," I said, "but what you think of my little stunt? Really didn't have to tell her. She more or less told herself."

"Doc phoned—" he said, as if he hadn't heard. He walked into the front room, behind the piano, looked at the spot. "Right here," he said to himself. "File 'em in, file 'em out."

"What's eating you, Captain?" I said. "What's on your mind?"

"Who—?" he said. "Me?"

"I've handled that little matter," I said. "What's eating you?"

"You tell her it was comin' here?"

"Sure—where else?"

He came back to the door at the front, peered through the glass.

"Would depend—" he said, "who she saw ridin' in it."

"We can take that for granted," I said. "After all, who else would it be?"

"That's where you're wrong?"

"Just what do you mean?"

He took a match from his vest pocket, chewed on it.

"You probably think I'm just a superstitious old fool—" he said.

"I don't know what to think," I said.

"Well—" he said, "you remember when she saw that danged wagon last night?"

"Of course——"

He didn't go. on. He faced the window, chewing the match.

"You told me she'd been seeing that wagon for thirty years——"

"Think she has. Always other people in it." Then he said, "Who's in the wagon is one way to put it. Another way to put it—" he turned and looked at me.

"Yes—?" I said.

"What were you sayin' yesterday—" he said. "That you were just passin' through?"

I nodded my head. "I guess I said that we were just passing through."

"Well, let's put it that way," said Purdy, came up and patted me on the arm, then walked through the front room and started up the stairs.

Put yourself in my shoes—standing there in that house, at the foot of those stairs, watching the old man, his hand on the bannister, slowly make the wide turn. When I tell you that I'm not a superstitious person, I've told you that I'm quite a bit like you are, so that I can leave you to reconstruct the scene for yourself. I stood below, in the hall, facing the flowers and the vacant square for the casket, the air warm and sweetish with the afternoon heat, the cigars, and the perfume. When I heard the old man finally quiet upstairs I crossed the room to the phone, steadied my hand, then asked the operator for the Bud Hibbard residence.

"You won't find either one of them there right now," Irene said.

"You mind ringing it, anyhow?" I said.

"Oh sure, I'll ring it."

On the tenth or eleventh ring the receiver went up.

"Hello—" said my wife.

I wiped my face with my sleeve, put out my free hand to the wall. "Hello Honey—" I said, inhaled, then said, "how are you and the kids?"

"You really want to know?"

I shook my head, gripped the wall again, said, "No."

"What's got into you?" she said.

"I just wondered," I said, "that's all. Isn't it all right for their father to wonder?"

"In a place where they might get killed any minute you never telephone, you never say a word, but when we get in a place like this—like this," she repeated, "why you call up and ask how we are."

"I just wondered," I said. "I just wanted to know."

"Well, we're still here," she said. "That make you feel better?"

"That's fine," I said. "That's just fine."

"But don't think we would be, for one moment, if we had that car."

"I'm on my way, Honey—" I said. "Right now. Just hold everything."

Her receiver went down, a little abruptly. I put down mine. When I turned to the room I saw the old man at the top of the stairs. His hat was off, and he rolled down his sleeves, buttoned them at the wrist.

"Well, I'm glad to see you use the phone—the facilities," he said.

"What's on your mind?" I said.

"You got a minute, Captain?" I nodded. "Just a minute is all—you can stand right there." I stood there and he went off into the room on his left. I heard him mussing around. "Well, here I come—" he said. I noticed that the sound of his walk was different, rather long and dignified, before he reappeared at the top of the stairs. He was wearing Clinton Hibbard's swallow tail, with the satin lapels. On his head was one of Clinton's bowlers—I had seen them as a boy—and the tails of the coat curved in between his bandy legs. Clinton Hibbard had been a man around six feet one, or two, and at the time he bought that coat about two hundred and ten pounds. "Would you say it was a little too loose, Captain?"

"Just a bit," I said, "if there was something you could do about the sleeves—" He nodded.

"How about the hat?"

"The hat's fine."

"You think she'd mind?"

"Why no—" I said. He felt better. He threw his shoulders back.

"I know how she'd *like* it to be," he said, "and we've got to make every effort to do it. It's our last chance, Captain," he said, "you realize that?"

I nodded, soberly.

"All right, Captain—" he said, "you can go now."

There were other things on my mind when I left the house, by the side door, so that I didn't notice Aunt Angie's door stood wide open. When she called— "Is that you Purdy?" I turned and saw her leaning on the ice box, her cane poking at the brace across the screen. When I stopped she peered over her glasses toward the door.

"No—this is Clyde, Aunt Angie?" I said.

"This is who?" I walked back to the door. As I stopped at the screen she said, "What you mean by sneakin' away?"

"I wasn't sneaking, Aunt Angie—my car's out there." I pointed across the yard, through the tomato poles.

"You an' your Uncle Irwin," she said, "pussyfootin' in the grass."

"What about my Uncle Irwin?" I said.

"You mean you don't know?"

"No, Aunt Angie," I said. Her eyes lidded, and her withered mouth closed in a wide, thin line. A cheshire smile. She opened her eyes and wheeled slowly, as if someone might be behind her, then she craned her head far to the right, back to the left.

"You won't let on I told you?"

"Heavens no—"

She sucked in her lip, fastened it down with her upper plate. After a moment she released the lip, sucked the plate inside.

"Your Uncle Irwin—" she said, "wasn't married. He went to the war."

"This is my father's Uncle Irwin?" I said.

"Hmmmm. I suppose it was. He didn't get married. He went off to the war. Gone seventeen months, twenty-three days. Your Uncle Billie was a boy, an' when he came back he asked your Uncle Irwin how it was." She turned once more to see how it was behind, peered around the yard. "Your Uncle Billie asked him, an' your Uncle Irwin said—fired two shots."

"He fired just two shots?"

"Your Uncle Irwin said he fired two shots. One at the enemy, one in his britches—his own britches." She wheeled around, her eyes lidded, blowing softly through her nose. Halfway across the kitchen she stopped, craned her head around slowly— "Now you won't let on I told you?"

"Not a word, Aunt Angie—" I said.

I walked off through the garden, walking in the sun before God and half the people in Junction, before I remembered where I had been, and what day it was. At the front of the house, under the heavy elms, and between the two stone hitching posts, Mr. Moody held a light green parasol high in the air. It had been over the woman at his side, but she had stepped forward to see me a little better, straining forward, like a dog on a leash. A uniformed chauffeur, his arms full of flowers, stood under the parasol. I raised my hand, the straining lady raised hers, the chauffeur nodded his head, bowed, and over them all, like a semaphore, Mr. Moody rocked the parasol. I walked through the sun, the weedy garden, and around to the shade side of my car.

At a time like this I like to sit down with a tall glass of iced coffee, but I can be persuaded, now and then, to take a substitute. Mabel's Lunch Room was one persuasion, the blinds drawn against the sun, and the thought of Nellie Hibbard was also a help.

I drove west along the tracks to where I could see the Hibbard house, the roof vibrating in the heat, and the dwarfed poplars, bent at the top like limp candles. I could also see my wife, on a straight chair in the kitchen to get away from the red plush seats, and the three kids stretched out for a nap on the linoleum floor. Later, much later, a fitful draft might be there.

I seemed to see all of this very clearly, the hot light caught in the net of the screen, and the steady drip from the cold water tap in the sink. Very clearly indeed, without any suggestion of fate, or imminent peril, or whatever it was I seemed to be feeling ten minutes ago. On hot afternoons Nellie would have the radio at her side—perhaps in the basement—and the peas she was shelling would make a wooden sound in the pan in her lap. Like clothespins, when she stirred them around. The sweet smell of the pods would be in the draft at the top of the stairs.

In such a house there was no place to explain imminent

peril. At four o'clock of a summer afternoon there was not much connection, on the surface, between the woman who had died, and the woman, or women, who had not. Later, there might be. But not at four o'clock. I made the first turn crossing the tracks and drove down the road, toward the tourist cabins, where the old Buick, with the sad-eyed dog, was parked out in front. The front door to the WEE BLUE INN was closed, the sign said Air-Coolt. I pushed on it and stepped inside, into the dark after the white glare of the road, and felt my way, my right hand out, toward a counter stool. I saw the white bar rag come and go, and in the bar mirror I could see the juke box, the red and yellow bubbles making their tireless way from tube to tube.

"An' yours, Bub—?" said the voice.

"I guess a bottle of Bud—" I said, and cooled my hands on the bar, then wiped them on my face. When I opened my eyes I could see the old man. He had taken off his hat, it sat beside him on the bar. The top of his head was the color of a flour sack, neither white nor yellow, but with a suggestion of the Pillsbury label coming through. He wiped the suds from his moustache, the long pull on his lip showing his brown teeth. Gazing at me soberly he said—"Favored by ladies an' gentlemen alike."

"What's that?" I said.

"Bottle of Bud—" he said, lifted his bottle, emptied it.

"Yes, it's damn good beer," I said, and tipped my glass. I let the beer trickle into it, cooling the edge of the glass.

"Tractor people—" went on the old man, picking up from wherever he had dropped it, "Caterpillar, think it was, came to me and said we like to show you a thing or two. Came to me, as head of the Commissioners. We would like to show you a thing or two, they says, and it's goin' to cost you nothin' but your time. You get on the train—" he pointed toward the door, "then you get off. Think his name was Leahy. Seemed a nice chap." He stopped for another swallow of beer, sprinkled the suds with salt. "So we went. Think there was eight or ten of us from right around here." He turned on the stool, put out his arm. "Had a car to ourselves, right up near the engine, picked up another car out of Omaha. They was Iowa Commissioners—they wanted to see the same thing. Meals in the Dining Car. All we had to do was to ask for it. Between meals, up an' down in the car, nice as girls you ever seen with whiskey an' wine. All dressed in black. Just their arms out. Arms as white as my head." He felt it. "My, they was jolly pretty things."

"Humph—" said the bar man.

"Says I, to one of them, think the purtiest one, which one them whiskies on that tray is imported?

"Im-ported? Why we makes our own whiskies. Right in Pee-oria.

"You don't say, says I.

"It's the water, she says. An' so it was. Seems they have what they call good whiskey water in Pee-oria." He took a swallow, then said, "We was in a Hotel, windows up front so you could see every which-way, auto-bus to come right to the door an' fetch us, pick us up. Had money. Nothin' we could do with it. You write a letter, one of these purty girls take it right out of your hand. Put a name on it for you. Put a stamp. Then take it away. There was nothin' too good for us, bed and board, everything was just dandy. We was there three days. Don't think I left the lobby at all. Town that size I'd just get myself lost, never find my way back."

"How was this tractor business?" I said.

"Guess it was all right. Don't remember much about it. Took us out one afternoon to see it workin'. Think we did. Then we was drove back to the lobby. Home the next night."

At the back of the bar, in the corner, a telephone rang.

"Who?" said the bar man, then, "Is it any my business what he has for a license? All right, all right, I'll ask him." He looked up. "Your name Muncy?"

"Yes—" I said.

"Would your wife be lookin' for ya?"

"Well, she might—" I said.

"What'll I tell her?"

"That's my wife?" I said.

"This's Mabel Potter."

"Tell her I'm on my way," I said.

"He says to say he's on his way. All right." He hung up. He came back down the bar, "If you wasn't new aroun' here I'd told you to park your buggy out in back. If it ain't that Potter, it's the goddam barber. Eyes like a hawk. There aint a goddam car in Loop county they don't know."

"Thanks, anyhow—" I said.

"Next time, just park it in back. No charge. Park it there any ole time you like."

"Many thanks," I said. I put a quarter on the counter, saw that it was twenty minutes past five. "Well, I'll be seeing you," I said, and nodded at the old man, who was looking right through me.

"Yes sireee—" he said, as I walked to the door, "they was jolly purty girls."

A sprinkler was running in the Swenson yard. As I drove by I thought I recognized the small white bottom, like a cork, seated on it, the legs drawn up so the water screened his face. At the back of the house, between the porch and the barn, Stephen B. Hibbard ran for cover, a Sherwin-Williams painter's hat on his head, but otherwise not a stitch. Young Hibbard, without his pants, was the spit and image of his father at the time we had gone in heavily for the same mysteries. We had tied it up with Indians, I seemed to remember, leaving all of our clothes in the grove of willows between the old cattle loader and the water stack. It made me wonder what they tied it up with now. Whether some city-boy, like my own, for the time being cooling on the water sprinkler, had been giving them the latest low-down on this fellow Freud. And if that was so, whether—yes, whether it was any longer possible for kids like young Hibbard and my own, to know some of the things I knew. Whether they would ever kiss Stella Conley, for instance, or whether they would know, at that moment, that this thing they were feeling was nothing more nor less than a foolish exaggeration of the love-object.

As I drove up in the yard, and shut off the motor, I could hear music—for my listening pleasure—coming from the basement window along the drive. I walked around to the rear door, entered the house. No one sat in the kitchen, the evening paper was spread across the table, and several coffee rings, old ones, sealed it to the oil cloth. An armful of sweet corn lay in the sink.

[166]

"Oh Nellie—?" I said.

"I'm down here, Clyde—" she said.

"How are you feeling, Nellie? You didn't go to town?"

"Oh, I'm all right Clyde, we got enough expenses as it is. By the time we take care of Mr. Moody, an' that coffin—" Her voice trailed off, the radio came on again.

"Where's Peg?"

"I think I heard her go in and lay down."

I went through the kitchen to the front room where the baby lay asleep, under a piece of cheesecloth, and I raised one corner, shooed out a fly.

"You want to feel if she's wet?" Nellie called. I felt.

"No, not yet—" I said.

As the sun had left the front of the house I raised the blind and looked out at the yard, the dust on my car, and the heavy dull nap of it on the lilac leaves. I opened the front door, to start a draft, and picked up the waybill that had been dropped there. I read of an Auction, July 19th, at the Kirsch Farm. A bead of sweat dropped from my face to a corner of the sheet.

"Are you coming, or aren't you?" my wife said. I put the waybill down on the piano and went into the bedroom, where the blinds were drawn, and my wife lay out with a towel on her forehead. A basin of water was on the floor at her side. "Wet it—" she said, and passed the damp towel to me. I rinsed it out, wiped my own face off, wet the towel again.

"Why don't you ask me if I wouldn't like an aspirin?" she said.

"Would you like an aspirin, dear?" I said.

"You want to kill your little wife with drugs?" she said. I waited. What fool was it who said to be forewarned, is to be forearmed? "Mrs. Nellie Hibbard—" my wife went on, "does not believe in the use of narcotics, ice cubes in water, Tampax, good or bad birth control, but she thinks that a nice fat steak is good for a black eye."

I looked around the room for the hot air radiator, it was under the bed. Music for my listening pleasure came through very well. I bent over to shut it off, then I thought better of it. In a loud voice I said— "Well, honey—she's sure a beauty now that she's dead."

My wife raised her wet head to look at me. I could see that she felt a good deal better already.

"They're really damn nice people," I said, "but you wouldn't know it, nobody knows it, until they kick the bucket, cross over to the better world. Then you can see it. You can see what really nice people they are."

As my wife's headache seemed to have passed I took off my shoes, wet the towel, and let her pack it on my own head as I lay back on the bed.

My eyes closed, I tried to reconstruct what had happened in the last twelve hours, since six A.M., when the old man had got me out of bed. I couldn't do it. Every event seemed a thing in itself. As remote from the next event as the epic ball game between St. Joe and Lincoln, or that second, and final shot, that Uncle Irwin had fired. Uncle Irwin's big shot, like Junction's, had been fired into his own britches, and that was where the stranger had to look for signs of it. Since morning I had been thumbing the loose pages of an old album, the pictures related, but the gist of the story getting out of hand. The Civil War pasted on the sheet with the WEE BLUE INN. Followed by Mr. Moody, a little tight in his vest, describing the features of a pine coffin, and incidentally dealing with the omit-flowers-dilemma at its source. Followed in turn by Mabel Potter and Aunt Angie, Chief Purdy, and by half of the once-proud population of Junction, arranged like iron filings around a magnet, Caddy Hibbard by name. All of them living in an arc, as boys will walk around a haunted house. Now that it had passed, and proved itself mortal, this strange force could be brought into the open, put in a satin lined gift box, and addressed familiarly. A kind of pressed flower, or a lock of scented hair, reminding the citizens of Junction that Life—with a capital—was not what it used to be. That once, if one could somehow believe it, they had been in love. Everybody, apparently, in particular those of whom one might least expect it, lifting the receiver to speak the word Caddy—familiarly. Yes, yes, they had all known her, intimately. They had passed in the evening, perhaps walking on the grass, at the edge of the curbwalk, to better hear the music—or lying near the window, like Mr. Lemuel Purdy, learning to sleep on the left side. In spite of all the noise, in spite of the lantern glow on one's face, and the street light blowing windy shadows, like voices, when the lanterns were out.

That light—wasn't that corner beacon at the heart of it? Right now waving over the dump, but when I was a boy—when we were all boys—pointing to the new world a-coming, the brave world we all had in mind. That light, and the new City Bank, went up the same year. This building was faced with fine Italian marble, imported for the better class banks and drug stores, but the sides and the back of the building were of plain red brick. It was naturally assumed that other structures would spring up, take care of this. And a year or so later one shop did, a fairly modest affair with a pressed-tin ceiling, a high false front, and a wooden awning over the walk. The left window was hung with a curtain and on the glass was the word

MILLINERY

and in the right window there was usually a cat and several bolts of cloth. The cat was usually asleep, and the bolts of cloth were generally obscured by the row of men, and their wide-brimmed straws, seated out in front. There were other places a man could sit—at the railroad station, for instance—but the older men had formed their sitting habits earlier. At that time the town was growing, and they liked to sit where they could watch it grow.

Around the turn of the century a man with good eyes, and a little spare time on his hands, could sit in his buggy, or on a bench in the square, and watch the town grow. Turning his head he could see the tower on the *finest edifice west of the Missouri,* not to mention the state's most promising educational institute. Like Miss Caddy's fine house, it was built out in the country, where it was quiet and not so crowded, and an example for the town that would grow up around it, any day now. Meantime, there was the Court House, a barn-red building three floors in height, with a flag waving, and a water tower that could be seen far out on the plains. Any man within sight of these towers, whether he liked them or not, whether willing or not, was part and parcel of the town in spite of himself. Part of the dream, part of this notion that was growing up. It all affected his life, in some way, leading him to think and to feel what he might not have been led to think or to feel at all. Some notion about himself, his children and the brave new world.

As these buildings were several years under construction every man in town, sooner or later, stopped under the awning to see how things were coming along. He watched them grow. He wondered, sometimes, if they would ever stop. Every man had some sort of stake in the future, as it happened that those who could sit and watch were not those, understandably, who had floated the bond. In this way, every man had a part in it. He had put his money in it, or his time, and when he stepped back under the awning, shading his eyes, it might be that he saw what he had hoped to see. A great future for himself, and a place for Caddy Hibbard's dream.

The town was up and coming—that is to say that it had this notion of being a big town, and the people in the town got to feeling this notion, to liking it. So it hung on, like the talk about a storm that everyone can see on the horizon, but somehow, for some reason or other, never turns up. Then one day, overnight almost, you miss something. You come to the screen, a towel in your hands, and look at the sky.

Perhaps a jerkwater town can't live with this notion of marble stairs, and those girls you used to see, Sunday evenings, in the tasseled lawn swings. Those girls had gone somewhere else, no doubt of it. They had gone to order meals that came in many parts, and leave a little food on all of the dishes, but nothing on the napkin but the bright color of their lips. They had gone to the cities, like my father, waiting for their name to be called in the lobbies, and for fruit to be served in a bowl of crushed ice. And they would like to know what you meant by this corn on the cob. In case you should ask them, they would like to know. And they would find all of these things, like Gatsby, because that was where they were driven, and because these things, like Gatsby, all came from the same place. They were born and raised right where you were, so to speak.

But when they grew up—well, perhaps they would miss something. That was hard to say, now that they had learned not to grow up. But it was still safe to say that sooner or later, on their way from some place to somewhere, they might drive off the road, off the main highway, to look for it. For the thing to remember, you see, is what you missed. That was what mattered. That was what you had been living with. That was why the old man across the tracks and his sad-eyed dog kept the lamp burning, and perhaps that was why I was back walking the streets. We didn't know much, but we knew we had missed something.

When my father built his city house out in the country there were plans for a park right across the road, and a fine bandstand with a pigeon roost on the roof. The block to the west had been surveyed and cut up into lots, the size of Miss Caddy's, and city sidewalks, with the ladies in mind, had been put in. But somehow, it didn't materialize. The population doubled, true enough, as most of the people had five or six kids, but while they were kids they all lived in the same house. And when they were not kids, when they were no longer youngsters, they moved away. Nothing much was done about that park as there were no kids to play in it, and the older folks had their own habits, their own backyards. The blocks that had been cut up for lots went back to grass. Some of the walks were not a total loss as there was a Chautauqua every fall, and over the summer a Circus and two or three carnivals. But there was always something foolish about the street light. Hanging where the crossroads had been planned, where the heavy city-traffic would demand it—a fine City lamp, giving a full view of the small town dump. On windy nights it swung back and forth, lighting up the pits where the garbage was burning, or Mr. Lemuel Purdy, lying awake in the room upstairs. The shade halfway up, as he had to keep an eye on the Hibbard house.

In front of the Hibbard house there were trees, with the big shade elms along the curbwalk, and closer in the white birches, and between the white birches the covered lawn swing. A yellow fringe, like a buggy tassel, around the top. Out in back was a garden, the rabbit hatch, a hammock purple with mulberry stains, and on long summer evenings you could hear the creak of the hammock ropes. Too many in it. There were always too many in Miss Caddy's swings. But now the lawn swings were rusty, the platforms matted with grass, and you could see where the hammocks had swung from the crease in the bark. For one day it was empty, and someone remembered to take it down. The street out in front was called Pioneer and the new street that crossed it was called Horace Greeley —but after mulling it over most of the boys had headed east. And the girls? They went where the boys were— naturally.

Naturally, but thirty years ago we had our place, we knew the points of the compass, and arranged ourselves in an orderly manner around an unseen force. Who had boasted of the fact that he was born and raised out here? What did that mean? I would say that it meant my compass was set. That however the world or the poles shifted, my needle still pointed toward the house on the corner where Miss Caddy Hibbard and Aunt Angie were known to live. A magnet, a north polar cap at the edge of Junction, supplying the town with energy and direction, like a dynamo. Perhaps this was why we walked around it like a haunted house. A force that might, at any time, blow the town up or leave it in darkness—but darkness was the thing that they feared. A great current had once passed through this town, with one pole in Miss Caddy, one pole in Aunt Angie, and one could string up a wire to this force and be alive. Anybody, all one had to be was there. Everybody, for one long day, had tapped in on it. They had passed of an evening, walking in the grass to better hear the wild, free voice of Miss Caddy, calling for music, for ice cream, for someone to stand up and dance. Or they had come to a window, like Mr. Purdy, so that the multicolored glow from the lanterns would warm their hands, the white flesh of their arms, and wave a shadow on the rug.

My wife shook me and said— "The phone. Don't you think you'd better answer it?"

I got up and walked across the kitchen, picked it up.

"This is me—" Bud said. "Don't think I'm going to make it for supper. You mind tellin' Nellie I'll be home around eight?"

"Sure," I said, "you'll be home around eight."

"You people stayin' another night?"

"No, we've got to get on," I said. "I was just telling Peg to round up the kids. We got to get on, plan to be in Iowa tonight."

"Well, you know your own mind. It's been good to see you," said Bud.

"It's been good to see you and Nellie, too—" I said.

"Next time," said Bud, "we won't get caught in a fix like this. We'll be in the big house by then. Have plenty of room."

"That'll be fine," I said.

"Be a different place when somebody is really livin' in it."

"Yes, I guess it will."

"An' say, Clyde, you mind tellin' Nellie that if she'd like to see the viewin' she can go with Mrs. Moody, who said so, or she can go with Auntie Lou. Mrs. Swenson said she'd keep an eye on the kids."

"I'll tell her."

"An' say, maybe you'd like to drop by yourself?"

"I doubt it, Bud——"

"Well, if you change your mind all you have to do is drop in. Say you're an old friend of the Hibbards. Nearly everybody was, if you go back far enough."

"I think we'll have to be getting on," I said.

"An' say—" said Bud, "I sure like your missus, say so now before I forget it. I didn't think the cities would produce a girl like that."

"Oh, they do," I said. "They do now and then."

"Nellie's pretty critical, but she likes her too."

"Well, many thanks——"

"I hope you didn't take what I said about city-kids too much to heart?"

"You know how I am," I said, "always been pretty sensitive."

"Nellie says city people never take criticism very well."

"She's a mighty sharp girl," I said, "and you're a lucky boy."

"We're both lucky," said Bud. "Think we can agree to that."

"Well, good luck, Bud—" I said. "I'll let you know when we're out this way again."

"Good luck, Clyde," he said, and hung up. I was still holding the receiver, facing the window, when it clicked several times.

"This Purdy," said the old man. "Thought I'd give you a ring." He stopped, and I could hear him shift the match around in his mouth. "Mrs. Moody was here, she and Mr. Moody. Put her in a nice summer dress. You never saw anything prettier in your life."

"That's fine, Captain—" I said, "that's just fine."

"We're openin' the doors in another twenty minutes—" I looked at the clock over the sink. Seven ten. "Thought maybe you'd like to run over before the crowd stomps in?"

"Can't make it, Chief," I said. "We've got to be on our way."

"Just a quick look, Captain?"

"I doubt it, Chief——"

"Let me talk to you straight, Captain—" he said, and I heard him spit out the match. "There's certain people who Caddy—you know what I mean—expects to be here. This your last chance, Captain, you know that." I didn't

[176]

answer and he said, "Well, anyways I want to thank you for all you did. Don't know what I'd done 'thout you around this afternoon." He paused, then said, "Want to thank you on her part, too."

"Glad to do it, Chief," I said, then realized that he had hung up.

"Sorry you're leavin' so soon," said the operator. "Any other number you'd like me to get?"

"No, no thanks—" I said, and put the receiver back on the hook.

"Oh Clyde!" It was Nellie. I walked around to the basement door. "Aren't you going to eat supper?" Dimly, in the twilight zone at the foot of the stairs, I saw Nellie. A towel was wrapped around her head, turban style. She pulled the ironing cord out of the iron, let it swing from the light.

"It's cool now, Nellie—" I said, "and we've got to reach the river before dark. You know how it is driving after dark on these country roads."

"We'll pick up a bite to eat along the way somewhere," my wife said.

"If everything just wouldn't happen all at once," Nellie said.

"Before something else happens," my wife said, "I want to get home." She walked to the front of the house, leaned out the window and called our kids.

"Now that I can understand," Nellie said. "I can understand that."

I picked up our bags and carried them out to the car. The day's work, whatever it had been, had taken the starch out of the boy, and he lay stretched out on his face in the back seat. That meant that his back was sunburned. A coating of Noxzema, like dried soap, covered the raw spot at the nape of his neck, and he clicked a green cricket from which most of the paint had been chewed.

I took a seat in the car on the chance that the boy, in spite of his glazed expression, might like to tip his father off on a few things. This sometimes happened when we had, so to speak, been through a good deal together, and found ourselves alone without the women to worry about. Did he have any feeling about empty corners, swinging street lights? Did this time in the evening, for example, seem to mean something private to him? A time when the lamps sparked in the hollow, and the red and green switch lights, far down the tracks, were without a glare and without shadows, quiet and framed. There was a time in the morning a good deal the same. There were lights, but without shadows—without, you might say, a past or a future, just passing the time until one of these prospects came along. Quite a bit like Junction, now that the current was off. Perhaps a town had to pass, like we did, from a shadowless morning to a shadowless evening, and perhaps Junction was now passing—before our eyes. From Aunt Angie through the Miss Caddy Hibbard line. Perhaps it then passed away, spreading itself like the Platte, with all of its meaning under the ground—out of sight but not quite out of mind. Would it reappear again, when the current came on?

I could see that Junction was a house divided, the old town facing the west and Horace Greeley, but the once up-and-coming part of town facing the east. For the east was the way out of town, the way to leave. To the east the town had lengthened like a shadow, the blurred edge crossing the fields, but to the west it ended abruptly on the sky. There was nothing to face. The windows of the Western Hotel were covered with blinds. The town not merely ended but the sky swept in, like a tide, to invade it, the flood of light and space lapping at the fringes, washing it away. The lawns had receded, the wooden walks, the slats of picket fences like a battered pier—was it any wonder one citizen should dream of the impending flood? The passing of all man-made things, the fatal careening of the globe? For whatever remained at this edge of town did so at a risk, and a bad one, as only the husk of several time-tired buildings remained. They faced to the west— a row of old men with their hands tied behind them, with blindfolded eyes—facing the firing squad, the careening globe, and the impending flood.

From the screen at the porch my wife called, "Come and tell Nellie good-bye, Clyde——"

I came to the screen and said, "Well, Nellie, I guess we're off."

From afar she said, "I hope you folks have a nice trip."

"If I'd had any idea," I said, "that you and Bud would ever sleep in that garage——"

"We often do it," she said, "it's just that there's more of 'em right now."

"Well," I said, "it won't happen again."

"Next time—" she said, in a firmer voice, "we'll have plenty room. We'll be over in the attic."

"The what?" my wife said.

"The attic—" said Nellie. "That's what Bud calls the Hibbard house."

"Well—" I said, "I suppose it is——"

"It's how you happen to feel about it," said Nellie.

"If we ever find a place big enough," said my wife, "we expect you to come and visit us."

"Someday—" said Nellie, "we want the children to see the Capitol."

"Well, you just let us know when—" I said, and came back to the car. My girl got in the front seat beside me, to make it clear she was one of *us*, and not a child anymore, with a silly sunburn, in the back seat. We sat there, listening to the voices coming through the basement window. Then it was quiet: the radio came on.

"Well, I guess that's *that*," she said, and her mother came out and got into the car. I backed out of the drive, heading the car east, and we went down the road past the Swensons' where a light was burning on the front porch.

"They're out—" my wife said, "is there something doing tonight?"

I might have answered that—I had my mouth open—but I noticed that my girl was staring at me, so I kept my face straight ahead, my eyes on the road. Perhaps that explained why I drove back into town. There was no need to drive through the town, I could have taken the first turn over the tracks—Tom Scanlon's crossing—but there we were on Pioneer street. There were lights out in front of many houses—both my women noticed that—before we saw the sight, like a house burning, at the end of the road. Down where the street light swung over the empty corner, and the smoking dump. Miss Caddy Hibbard's place was lit up—as they used to say—like a barn dance, the shutters thrown open, and lights in every room in the house. From several blocks away it looked like a fire raging inside. It lit up the nickel on the parked cars, the brass fitting on several teams of mares, buggy weights in the ditch grass, and here and there it sparked an old man sitting it out. His feet on the buckboard, the reins idle in his hands. Other reins were looped around the whip posts, or dangling loose, so the horse could graze in the long ungrazed grass edging the road. Behind the curtained windows I could see the people milling around. Several ladies stood on the porch, and from a third floor window, her nose pressed to the glass, a woman cupped her hands to her face and peered below. She wagged her head from side to side at what she saw.

"What in the world is going on—" my wife said, "a wedding?" I made the turn at the corner, parked at the side of the house. There was no music, no lanterns on the lawn, no voice screaming at the tailless donkey, but otherwise it was quite a bit like old times. The music would begin, I was sure, as soon as the refreshments were served. Caddy Hibbard would step out on the porch and wave her thin arm, like her finger had been bitten, and several young men would hurry forward to examine it. One of them remaining, like a sentry, at her side. A man was always needed. They were easily found. Perhaps a candle had burned the colored paper in a lantern, or the melting wax, just as she was passing, dropped a lover's kiss—as she called it—on her gloved hand. Time would be called while this was looked into, then wound up again——

"Well, honey—" I said, "the old man wanted me to stop and look in."

"You mean to tell me—" she said, then turned from me to look at the house, the flaming windows. One went up. A man's arm parted the curtains for a draft.

"This is it," I said, "this is Nellie Hibbard's attic."

"The old lady," she said, "—isn't there an old lady?"

"She's out in back," I said, "in the lean-to." I pointed to the rear of the house where a lamp glowed behind a green blind. I could just make out the shape of the bird-box against the light. "She uses a lamp," I said, "she doesn't like the new order much."

"Is she back there—now?"

"I suppose so——"

"Doesn't she know what's going on?" I shrugged my shoulders. "You mean to say none of you people even told her?"

"She's a very old lady, now—" I said. "These things take time."

"Honest to God—" my wife said. "I'll go tell her myself."

"Don't get so excited," I said. "I went around to tell her. I think she knows."

"What do you mean—you *think* she knows?"

"It's a complicated story—" I said. I reached for my raincoat in the back seat. "I'd better just look in. Tell the old man good-bye."

"You're not doing a thing until you explain what you mean."

"What needs to be explained?" I said.

"This hokey-pokey business," she said. "If you haven't really told her, why you can go do that now. What in the world would she think—hearing all of this racket in her empty house?"

"She's pretty deaf," I said, "and besides——"

"Either you go and tell her—or I will." She looked

at me. "No, I don't trust you, I'm going to tell her myself." She opened the door before I got a hold of her.

"Whoops-a-daisy," I said, "suppose you hear my story first?"

"Only if you make it snappy."

I leaned back in the seat. In the rear-view mirror I could see my boy's sunburned face. He was awake now, his eyes were wide. Things were looking up.

"Well, go on—" said Peg.

"I tried to tell you last night," I said, "but you were full of your own story."

"I had other things to think about. Plenty of them."

"Well—" I said, "to make a long story short, I went over this afternoon—to tell her. Purdy asked me. He didn't want to do it himself. As I say, I went over with every intention of———"

"Just what I thought," Peg said. "You didn't. I will."

"Will you let me explain it?"

"Let Daddy explain," my boy said.

"As I tried to tell you last night," I said, "Aunt Angie has been too long by herself. When you do that you live your own life. You begin to see things———"

"Will you stop beating around the bush?"

"Well, last night we got to talking—Purdy, the old lady, and I—when I noticed she was sitting there mumbling to herself. Then she leaned forward, as if to look out the window, and said, 'There it goes—there it goes!'"

"There goes what?"

"Well, that's the story," I said. "She's got this habit of seeing things go by in the street."

"If you don't tell me what this thing is———"

"All right—" I said, "just remember you asked for it."
I looked around at them, then I said, "*The Dead Wagon.*"

"The what?"

"The Dead Wagon. That's what the old lady is in the habit of calling a hearse." My wife sat there. "Well, you asked for it," I said.

"What is so wrong if she does——"

"Nothing at all," I said, "I'm telling you what she saw out the window—and that Caddy Hibbard also lived in that house." They looked at it. Then they turned back and looked at me. "To get on with my story," I said, "when I stopped in to see her this afternoon—" I paused there, "she leaned out the window and saw this Dead Wagon again. Is that clear—" I said, "or you want me to explain?"

"Are you trying to frighten your own children?"

"We asked for it, didn't we?" said the boy.

"That's right, son—" I said, "and I hate to keep a good yarn to myself."

"That's enough," said Peg, "you can go now."

"There's just one more little point—" I said. "After I got away from Aunt Angie, Purdy and me had a little chat. I asked Purdy how it was that this Dead Wagon business seemed to please the old lady. She got a kick out of it."

"Go on—" said the boy.

"Purdy said that depended on who she saw ridin' in it." I stopped there to let that sink in. "I took it for granted, I said, that who she saw ridin' in it would be Caddy. You think I'm a superstitious old fool, he said? I don't know, I said, I don't know what to think. Well, he said, there's another way to put it. Put it this way——"

The boy got up from the seat, leaned over to look at my face.

"What were you saying—Purdy said to me—about just passing through? That's all we're doing, I said, and glad of it. Well, he said to me, say we put it that way—and then he walked off." Just as the old man did to me I patted my wife on the arm, my boy on the head, and gave my little girl a squeeze. "Suppose you think that over," I said. "I'll be right back."

Now I'm not much of a story-teller, but with that house in the yard behind me, the windows lit up, not a great deal remained to be said. On the face of my wife I could see that I had said enough.

"Well, think it over, folks," I said, and feeling pretty good about myself, and not at all superstitious, I started across the yard. Passing a wide open window, I slowed down for a peek at the room.

I often wonder what might have happened to me if I had walked on by. If I hadn't behaved more or less normal, and peeked from the yard. I might have seen Caddy Hibbard, for one thing, something I had really failed to do as a boy, and this might have done for me what other things failed to do. Cleared up the little problem of which way, if any, the life of Junction was now facing, or if it was Junction, rather than Caddy Hibbard, who had died. As it is, I have to go on guessing at these things. I had a look through the window, but I didn't get into the house. As this window stood open, the curtains parted, I could see across the room that she called the parlor to the flower-stacked piano, the line of viewers, and the casket on wheels. I caught a glimpse of this casket—one of Mr. Moody's best, with the wood stained to look like a doorknob, and the pink satin stuffing, oozing out of the top as if it were squeezed. The lower lids were closed—but not quite—like a lady's suitcase before it is sat on, the pretty underthings, of pink and white, sticking out of the cracks. I saw all this at a glance, as the line was moving, the procession of viewers facing away, except for Mabel Potter, who had turned to look at something. Something she had heard, as her round moon face, dull with powder, was still out of focus, and her mouth slightly open, as if that would help. What she had heard, what she now strained to see, stood between Mabel Potter and the parlor, in the band of darkness between the two crowded, light-blind rooms. In the wide hall that led to the rear, where there were steps going down to the basement, or through the pantry to the bolted kitchen door. Closed, it was said, for a good many years, but Mabel Potter, standing there among the fresh-cut flowers, just left of the piano, had heard something and turned to see what it was. Above the whispering in the room, the steps on the stairs, the voices that curved around the bend of the landing, she heard a tapping in the hall and before she looked she knew what it was. Knowing what she knew, half the people in Junction might have done the same. For after all, this was the Hibbard house, known to contain one Angeline Hibbard, and a Miss Caddy Hibbard who was reported to be dead. So that what one heard, or what one saw in the hallway, was more or less clear.

Aunt Angie Hibbard had come to the viewing herself. She stood framed in the wide, arched doors so that we both saw her in profile, her legs wide spread, a loose apron dangling from her neck. An old bear at the front of her cave, with the light from a forest fire there before her, showing the thin patch of hair on her head, her feeble legs. She had heard the commotion, perhaps she had seen the lights on the lawn. Perhaps once more she had heard that Dead Wagon creak in the road, make the turn at the corner, and drive right up—as she knew it would—beside the house. The front of the house, where the lanterns had once hung. So that after thirty years the time had come to take the key from the bowl in the cupboard, open the kitchen door, and walk from the back to the front of the house. From the old world, that is, into the new one. And now that she was there she faced the light, Mabel Potter, and the flowers on the piano; then she slowly craned her head to where they were gathered, like a choir, on the stairs.

"That you Purdy?" she said, but nobody answered. Naturally. Nobody answered, nobody moved, until she moved, her pointed heels dragging, and stepped from the narrow band of darkness into the light. Then they fell away from the front of the piano, backed away from the wall. The long line from the front door to the coffin frazzled at each end, like a string burning, then curled up sharply to a knot of faces behind the flowers. From the landing—loose in the long sleeves and hanging tails of Clinton Hibbard's coat—Mr. Purdy saw that her bloomers were showing through the seat of her dress. Then he was there at her side—but she would have none of him. Not a word—she waved him off—but while her cane was still in the air she saw the light on the polished coffin hardware, the satin frothing at the top. That was all she could see, just the hardware, the highlights glistening like so many doorknobs, brassy and green, like the worn trim on a nickel watch. But that was enough—that was just as she knew it would be. Her cane wagged, she made a soundless rattle as if some fool squirrel was in the box there before her, and Mr. Purdy seemed to think she was going to rap on it. Rattle her cane until whatever it was had left. He put out his hand, and she whacked him one-two-three right across the knuckles, threatened to spank him, then shooed him off. The floor to herself, she wheeled around and started back. Once more Mr. Purdy would help her and she had to threaten him, shoo him off again, and wag her cane at the silent gathering on the stairs. Facing them, her apron blowing in the draft down the stair well, she felt again what she had known all the time. The folly of it. They were witless. And now they were dead.

In the morning the Dead Wagon would come and for the first and last time put an end to the witlessness of all these years. They were dead. It was time to bury them. She cracked the floor once, twice, with her cane, then slowly moved into the hallway, into the darkness, and before Mr. Purdy stirred himself she was out of sight. He came to stand between the folding doors, gazing after her. The cuffs of Clinton Hibbard's sleeves rested in his hands as if in this manner he supported the coat, the round sagging shoulders, and the head balanced at the top. The soft chin tapped down on the pointed collar tips.

Purdy was still there, peering down the hallway, when I turned from the window and walked my long shadow back to the car. Perhaps I looked like a man who had seen something. Whatever it was, my wife said nothing, my two city-bred kids said nothing, and in the soft quiet I started the motor, backed out to the road. I tipped the rear-view mirror to keep the light out of it. On Greeley street I turned to the left for Tom Scanlon's crossing, east of Junction, and just a block down the road from the WEE BLUE INN. The old man's Buick, with the sad-eyed dog, was there in the yard.

"I've been thinking—" my girl said, "you want to know what I've been thinking?"

Nobody did. It was more or less clear, I guess, to all of us.